The moment Rachel gave in and began to skip, her joy took flight. Her skirt skimmed her calves, and her dark hair swung and shimmered with every hop.

She suddenly realized her inattention was a mistake, because a large figure loomed in her path. She tried to dodge. Momentum foiled the effort. She smashed into a man's broad, solid chest with a thump and a stifled screech.

The boxes of crayons and loose drawing paper she'd been carrying sailed into the air. The whole mess rained down on them. Crayons rolled all over the sidewalk, making solid footing nearly impossible.

"Look out!" the man shouted belatedly.

Everything happened so fast, it took Rachel a few seconds to realize why she hadn't fallen when they'd collided. Her blue eyes widened and focused on the stranger whose warm, strong hands were clamped on her upper arms, steadying her....

Books by Valerie Hansen

Love Inspired

VALERIE HANSEN

was thirty when she awoke to the presence of the Lord in her life and turned to Jesus. In the years that followed she worked with young children, both in church and secular environments. She also raised a family of her own and played foster mother to a wide assortment of furred and feathered critters.

Married to her high school sweetheart since age seventeen, she now lives in an old farmhouse she and her husband renovated with their own hands. She loves to hike the wooded hills behind the house and reflect on the marvelous turn her life has taken. Not only is she privileged to reside among the loving, accepting folks in the breathtakingly beautiful Ozark Mountains of Arkansas, she also gets to share her personal faith by telling the stories of her heart for Steeple Hill's Love Inspired line.

Life doesn't get much better than that!

SAMANTHA'S GIFT

VALERIE HANSEN

Published by Steeple Hill Books™

STEEPLE HILL BOOKS

Steeple
Hill®

ISBN 0-373-87224-0

SAMANTHA'S GIFT

Copyright © 2003 by Valerie Whisenand

Visit us at www.steeplehill.com

Printed in U.S.A.

For He shall give his angels charge over thee,
to keep thee in all thy ways.

—Psalms 91:11

My sister Audrey has suggested that I dedicate this book to our mother, Helen Hansen, who was a stickler for correct spelling and grammar, and probably taught me a lot more than I cared to admit, especially in my student days. Mom was also the one who laid the foundation of faith by taking us to Sunday school. So this one's for her. I wish she were here to read it.

Chapter One

Rachel Woodward's spirits soared the moment she stepped out the supply room door into the clear, warm Ozark morning. Pausing in appreciation, she took a slow, deep breath of fresh mountain air, noted the spicy, familiar aroma of the crayons and colored construction paper piled high in her arms, and smiled.

Another day in paradise. Life was as close to perfect as it could get.

Working with young children and seeing the world through their eyes made Rachel feel as if she were discovering new wonders every day. Their innocent enthusiasm was contagious. Why, if she were six instead of twenty-six, she might even give in to the urge to skip happily down the sidewalk all the way to her classroom!

She clasped the stack of supplies closer to her chest

and looked around furtively. Did she dare? What would it hurt as long as no one saw her? Few students arrived this early in the morning and the other teachers were either in the staff lounge discussing their summer vacations or already in their rooms finishing last-minute preparations. The coast was clear.

Rachel's grin widened. Why not? It seemed like a sin to suppress all the elation she was feeling, simply because society dictated that adults should behave more sedately.

Who wanted to be a stuffy adult, anyway? Certainly not *her.*

The moment she gave in and began to skip, her joy took flight. Her skirt skimmed her calves and her shoulder-length dark hair swung with every hop.

Squinting against the bright sunshine, she blinked slowly, reverently. *Thank you, Father, for finding me a job that blesses me so much.*

That instant's inattention was a mistake. A large figure loomed suddenly in her path! She tried to dodge. Momentum foiled the effort. She smashed into a man's broad, solid chest with a *thump* and a stifled screech.

Boxes of crayons and loose drawing paper sailed into the air. The whole mess rained down on them. Crayons rolled all over the sidewalk, making a solid footing nearly impossible.

"Look out!" he shouted belatedly.

Everything happened so fast that it took Rachel a

few seconds to realize why she hadn't fallen when they'd collided. Her vivid blue eyes widened and focused on the stranger whose warm, strong hands were clamped on her upper arms, steadying her.

Since Rachel was barely five-foot-two and slight, she'd often found herself at a size disadvantage. This instance, however, was much worse than usual. This man was so tall, so broad shouldered, so obviously muscular, she felt like the captive of a giant. Hopefully, a *friendly* one.

Her mouth suddenly went dry. Heart pounding, she fought to catch her breath and compose herself in spite of the nervous fluttering in her stomach. She knew it was normal for people to feel a surge of adrenaline when they were startled the way she'd just been, but this was ridiculous. She was not one of those faint-of-heart women who swooned every time an attractive man looked her way.

And speaking of looking… The man's chest, covered in a pale shirt and navy blazer, fell at her eye level. Following the line of his tie upward she saw a square jaw, firm mouth, hazel eyes—and an expression clearly filled with amusement.

She was too embarrassed to mirror his good humor. With a stubborn lift of her chin she did her best to appear unruffled as she asked, "Where did *you* come from?"

"Cleveland." A half smile lifted one corner of his mouth.

"I meant just now," Rachel told him. "I didn't see a soul in the hall before you ran into me."

"*I* ran into *you?*"

"Yes." She tried unsuccessfully to pull away. When he continued to hold on to her, she asserted her independence clearly. "That's enough. You can let go of me now."

"Okay."

The man released her so abruptly, she staggered and almost wound up sitting at his feet amid the spilled crayons. Wouldn't *that* have been cute! As if being caught skipping wasn't bad enough.

"I didn't mean for you to throw me down," she said.

"Make up your mind." He stuffed his hands into the pockets of his slacks and struck a nonchalant pose.

Rachel studied his face and frowned, trying to place him. "Who are you, anyway?"

Watching the movement of her eyes, he must have guessed that she was casting around for something with which to write; he stooped and came up with a blue crayon and a piece of the drawing paper she'd dropped.

"I'm Sean Bates. But you don't have to bother reporting me, ma'am. I work here."

"You do?" She paused, crayon poised. "Since when? I didn't see you at the in-service meetings last week."

"That's because I just moved from up north."

"You really are from Cleveland? It wasn't a joke?"

He laughed. "Not to me."

So, this was the new school counselor she'd heard so much about. No wonder all the single women on staff were figuratively lining up to vie for his attention. He was not only good-looking, he had a charisma that was almost irresistible—to anyone but her, of course. She wasn't susceptible to that kind of romantic insanity anymore.

Smiling up at him, Rachel said, "Well then, welcome to Serenity Elementary. If I can be of any assistance, please let me know."

"Thanks. I do have one question."

"Sure. Anything."

"Okay. Why were you skipping down the hall like a kid?"

"Shh." She blushed, looked around furtively. "You weren't supposed to notice that."

"It was kind of hard not to."

"Then, why didn't you get out of my way?"

"I tried. Guess I was so surprised, I didn't move quite fast enough. Sorry."

"Me, too." Pulling a face, she lamented the supplies scattered at their feet, then gathered the hem of her skirt at her knees, holding it bunched in one hand so she could crouch down safely. "My poor crayons. They were brand new. I'll bet half of them are broken."

Sean squatted to help her gather up the spill. "Hey, these are those big fat crayons. I haven't seen any of those since kindergarten."

"Makes sense. That's what I teach."

"You're a teacher?"

"Yes, I'm a teacher. Why?"

"No special reason. You don't fit my memories of the teachers I had when I was a boy, that's all."

Rachel knew better than to acknowledge the back-handed compliment and open their conversation to more of his personal opinions. There was nothing he could say about her diminutive appearance that she hadn't heard many times before.

She continued to stack paper, barely glancing at him. "Do you have children coming to our school, too, Mr. Bates?"

"No. No kids."

The answer was simple. It was the off-putting tone that drew and held her attention. The man had sounded as if he didn't even like children, which was a definite drawback since he was about to start a job where he'd be up to his elbows in them.

"You *are* the new counselor, aren't you?"

"Yes."

Silent, she studied his profile, trying to determine if she'd read him correctly. He looked to be about thirty or thirty-five, with reddish brown hair and compelling green eyes.

He raised them to meet hers. "What?"

"Nothing. I was just wondering what brought you to a little town like Serenity. Being from the city, you're liable to have quite an adjustment to make."

"I'll cope. It wasn't a spur-of-the-moment decision." Straightening with an armload of loose supplies, he changed the subject. "Lead the way to your room, Teacher. I'll carry these for you."

"I can manage by myself."

"I know you can." He lifted an eyebrow. "I just had a demonstration of how well. But I've already got this stuff balanced. If I try to hand it to you and you fumble it again, you'll have even more busted crayons. Let's go."

That logic overcame Rachel's misgivings. She gathered up the last of the paper and started off. "Okay. Come on. I'm in building A. You may as well start learning the layout of the campus. Where's your office, anyway?"

"So far, I don't have one."

"I'm not surprised. We aren't used to having a full-time counselor on staff."

"I'm not exactly full time. Not yet. I've told the boss I can fill in as a substitute bus driver, too, if they need me."

Confused, she glanced back over her shoulder at him. "Bus driver? Why? I thought you were a psychologist."

"Hey, I'm a versatile guy."

"If you say so." She paused to unlock the door to

her classroom, then pushed the door open with her hip and swept through ahead of Sean.

"I do say so." He cast around for the best place to dump his load of crayons and settled on the top of a low cabinet. "Actually, I put myself through college by driving a school bus."

She studied him further, frowning and questioning her deductions regarding his age. "How long did that take?"

Sean laughed. "It's a little complicated. Let's just say that counseling wasn't my first career."

"Hmm. I was sure I wanted to be a teacher from the time I was seven," Rachel said.

"I envy you. Most people aren't that decisive, even as adults."

He looked her up and down as he spoke. She was petite, pretty, and so thin she looked like she'd blow away in a strong wind—unless she happened to be tethered to the jungle gym. When he'd steadied her in the hallway, he'd noticed that he could easily encircle her upper arm with one hand. Good thing she'd chosen to teach very young children. The thought made him smile.

"What's so funny?"

"Sorry. I was just thinking." His gaze traveled around the room. "Kindergarten was a good choice."

"Why? Because children are so loving at that age?"

"No. Because you don't look like you could hold

your own in a pillow fight against anybody much bigger."

Rachel's smile faded. "You'd be surprised what I can do." She hustled him to the door, opened it and practically shoved him through. "Thanks for your help, Mr. Bates. Now, if you'll excuse me, I have a lot of work to do before class starts."

"Sure. No problem. Have a good day."

Rachel closed the door behind him and leaned against it, eyes shut tight.

Not hold her own? Ha! She might not look tough on the outside, but inside she knew she was made of steel. Tempered steel. And the pain of the tempering process lingered. It probably always would.

An unexpected call summoned Rachel to the office right after the dismissal bell. She was anything but thrilled. The first few days of every school year were very tiring, and the last thing she wanted was to have to face the principal this late in the afternoon. Refusal, however, was not an option.

Sean was coming out of a classroom as she passed by. He beamed at the sight of her. "Hi."

"Hi. So far, so good?" Rachel asked pleasantly, trying to ignore the jolt of awareness she'd felt the moment she spied him again.

"No problems," Sean said.

"Good."

"You okay? You look kind of funny."

Did her unwarranted reaction show? Oh dear! Hedging, she made a silly face at him. "Thanks—I think."

"Actually, you remind me a lot of a condemned man on the way to the gallows."

"Oh, that." *What a relief.* "Probably because I feel like one. I've been called to Principal Vanbruger's office and I don't have the slightest idea why. That kind of thing always gives me butterflies in my stomach."

"Is there a problem?"

"Who knows. It's a little too early in the year for me to have earned a commendation for exemplary teaching, so I have to assume that's not why he wants to see me."

"You never know. Maybe you're about to get a blue ribbon for your skipping skills."

"Let's hope not."

He fell into step beside her. "I'm headed your way. Mind if I walk along? Keep you company?"

"Aren't you afraid to be associated with a terrible rule-breaker like me?"

"Not as long as I don't catch you running with scissors," he quipped. "I do have my limits."

"Glad to hear it."

Rachel couldn't help chuckling softly. The man seemed to have the kind of nature that lifted a person's spirits. That quality made him more appealing to her than any superficial attributes, like the fact that he was every bit as handsome as her friends had insisted during lunch, when she'd carelessly mentioned having met him.

She and Sean reached the door to the school office. Rachel paused. "Well, this is it. Here I go."

"Want me to hang around till you're done?"

She was amazed at his sensitivity. "No. I'll be fine. I just hate the idea of hearing that I'm not perfect."

Sean arched an eyebrow. "I don't know. You look pretty good to me. Tell you what. If that guy Vanbruger picks on you, tell me, and I'll go let the air out of the tires on his bicycle so he knows better the next time."

Amused, Rachel looked up into his kind face and caught a glimmer of deeper concern. He'd apparently been trying to distract her with his silly banter and was now waiting to see if he'd been successful.

She assumed a pseudo-serious expression, made a fist and punched him lightly in the upper arm as she said, "Thanks, buddy. It's good to know you're standing by in case I need avenging. But I don't think he rides a bicycle, so that's out. Guess I'll just have to take my chances."

Turning, she reached for the doorknob. So did Sean.

His hand closed gently over hers. Their inadvertent touch sent tingles zinging up Rachel's arm and prickled in the tiny hairs at the nape of her neck.

She quickly slipped her hand from beneath his,

hoping he couldn't tell how bewildered her unexpected, fervent response had left her. Or how close
she'd come to actually shivering just now!

"Allow me," Sean said, gallantly opening the office door for her and stepping back with a bow.

Rachel took a deep breath and held it. She sidled
through the open door without looking up or glancing
back at Sean. Principal Vanbruger wasn't the main
reason for her nervousness anymore. Sean Bates was.

Not only were her original butterflies still having a
riotous party in her stomach, but the moment Sean
had accidentally touched her hand, they'd invited all
their friends—and a few hundred moths, to boot!

Rachel's bumfuzzled state of mind became of sec-
ondary importance the moment she entered the principal's office and saw who, and what, was waiting for
her.

Her gaze lingered a moment on the two adults, then
went to a withdrawn-looking little girl sitting on a
chair in the corner, lower legs and feet dangling.

The child's shorts and T-shirt were faded and much
too big for her, but that wasn't the saddest part. Everything, from her posture to her placement in the
room, screamed *lonely,* immediately capturing Rachel's heart.

Principal Vanbruger rose from behind his desk.
"Ah, good. Ms. Woodward, I believe you know Ms.

Heatherington, from Health and Human Services in Little Rock.''

Rachel nodded. ''Yes.'' She shook the social worker's hand formally. ''We've met.''

He gestured toward the child. ''And this is Samantha Smith. Samantha, this is your new teacher, Ms. Woodward.''

''Please, call me Miss Rachel,'' she told the shy little waif. ''All the other children do.'' Wide, pale blue eyes stared up at her from a cherubic face surrounded by unkempt blond curls.

Approaching slowly and pausing in front of the child, Rachel said, ''I see we're all out of my favorite kind of chair. Can I share yours? I'm pretty little. There should be room for both of us.''

Samantha's only answer was to scoot to one side. Rachel perched on the edge of the seat at an angle and laid her arm across the chair's low, curved back. That not only helped her balance, it formed a pose of guardianship, offering unspoken protection in a world of staid, intimidating adults.

''Samantha's parents died,'' the social worker said. ''She's in foster care right now. I'm working on getting her placed with relatives in Colorado, so I doubt you'll have to bother with her for long. She hasn't been behaving very well, I'm afraid. Just try to keep her out of trouble and make the best of it till the paperwork comes through and we can send her out of state.''

Tactful, as always. Rachel wanted to jump up and scream, *How dare you be so matter-of-fact? Can't you see how frightened the poor thing is?*

Instead, Rachel settled back into the chair, lowered her arm and pulled the little girl against her as if they were already fast friends. The glare of animosity she sent across the room belied her casual posture.

"I can read all the details in the files later, Ms. Heatherington. There's no need to discuss any of it now."

Without waiting for a reply, Rachel leaned down and whispered in Samantha's ear, then stood, holding out her hand. "If you'll excuse us—we're going to see my classroom."

The social worker opened her mouth to object and was silenced by the righteous anger in Rachel's backward glance.

"I'm going to show Samantha the playground, too. Then she'll know where everything is when she gets here tomorrow."

Wisely, Principal Vanbruger shooed them on their way with a wave of his hand and a firm "Fine. Go. I'll take care of things here."

Rachel was thankful he had interceded. If she'd been forced to stay in that woman's presence much longer she was afraid she might have expressed a very un-Christian opinion. That wouldn't do. It was bad enough to be thinking it in the first place.

Chapter Two

Proceeding down the sidewalk to the double doors that would take them to the interior halls of one of the low, nondescript buildings, Rachel kept up a friendly banter.

"It's not far to my room. Here we are. Look. First you go in these glass doors by the big letter *A*." Pointing, she led the way. "Then you find the room with a green door. It's right here. See the *K* on it? That stands for *Kindergarten*. I put a smiley face in the window, too, so all the kids can be sure this is the right place. Can you see that?"

The five-year-old nodded solemnly.

"I like to smile big like that. It makes my whole face happy," Rachel said as she reached for the door-knob. "Let's go inside and see where your seat is going to be. I have new crayons and pencils for you, too.'' She felt the child's grip on her hand tighten. ''Do you like to draw and color?''

Another nod.

''Good. Me, too.''

Rachel swung the door open and ushered her new student into the colorfully decorated classroom. One whole wall was plastered with letters of the alphabet, arranged amid the flowers and vegetables of a cartoon-like garden. In the foreground, a bunny made of the letter *B* was nibbling on a carrot that was bent to resemble a *C*. On the opposite side of the room there was a sink, bookcase and bright blue cabinet with banks of cubbyholes. Red, blue and yellow plastic chairs surrounded four low, round work tables and echoed the same vivid colors.

Above the chalkboard, Rachel had fastened gigantic numbers, one through ten, and a more sedate version of the *ABC*s. No flat, vertical surface remained undecorated. It had taken days to pin the pictures and cutout letters to the bulletin boards. Judging by the look of amazement and awe on the child's face, the effort had been well worth it.

''Did you go to preschool?'' Rachel asked.

''Uh-uh.''

She talked! *Thank You, God!* Rachel felt like cheering. Instead, she kept her tone deliberately casual. ''That's okay. We'll learn our letters and numbers here in my class, together.''

''I'm five,'' Samantha said softly.

"I'm a little older than that," Rachel countered with a grin.

"Teachers are supposed to be old."

"That's right. You're very smart."

The child beamed. "I know."

At least she hasn't lost her sense of self-worth, Rachel mused. That was a big plus. Obviously, someone in Samantha Smith's past had done a wonderful job of making her feel worthwhile. That confidence would help her adjust to whatever troubles came her way, the loss of her parents being the worst one imaginable. It was hard enough growing up *with* parents, let alone coping without them.

Except maybe in the case of my own mother. The thought popped into Rachel's head before she had time to censor it. There were some people who could give advice in a way that made the recipient glad to follow it. Then there was Rachel's mother, Martha. When Martha Woodward spoke, she acted as if everyone should be thrilled to profit from her superior wisdom. To disagree with her opinions was to invite condemnation. Rachel was, unfortunately, very good at doing that.

As she reflected on the strange twists and turns her private life had taken lately, she stood aside and watched the curious child explore the classroom. The sight brought a smile and a sigh of contentment. Teaching was Rachel's God-given gift and she relished every moment of it. Moreover, when she got a chance to help an emotionally needy child like Samantha, even for a short time, the blessing was magnified.

Rachel hoped that someday, if she was patient enough, Martha would finally accept the fact that her only daughter was single by choice. That her happiness came from loving other people's children as if they were her own.

If that happened, it would be a direct answer to prayer. And if not? Well, that would be an answer of another kind, wouldn't it?

The playground was deserted when Rachel finally took Samantha outside to the play equipment. It was grouped according to size. That which was assigned to the youngest children was naturally the smallest. The stiff, canvaslike seats of those swings were so tiny that even a person as diminutive as Rachel couldn't fit into them safely. Knowing that, she led the way to the next larger size.

Samantha strained on tiptoe to make herself tall enough to scoot back into one of the higher swings.

Rachel sat next to her and pushed off with her feet, swinging slowly, as if they were simply two friends sharing a recess. "I like to do this, don't you?"

"Uh-huh." Because she could no longer reach the ground, the little girl wiggled and kicked her feet in the air, managing to coax very little back and forth motion out of the swing. "Will you push me?"

"Okay. But first, watch how I move my legs. See? I pull them in when I go backward, then lean back and stick them out to go forward."

The child made a feeble try, failed, and pulled a face. "It doesn't work."

"It will. You just need to practice. Watch again. See?"

Instead of listening, Samantha jumped down and stalked away, kicking sand and muttering to herself, "Dumb old swing. I hate swings."

So much for the buddy system, Rachel thought. It served her right. She'd taken one look at Samantha Smith, sensed her loneliness, identified with her, and promptly broken her own rule against blurring the line between teacher and pupil.

"Okay. Fun's over," she said. "Time for you to go back to the office so Ms. Heatherington can drive you home."

Samantha whirled. "No!"

"Yes." Rachel cocked her head to one side, raised an eyebrow and held out her hand. "Come on."

Tears blurred the little girl's wide, blue eyes. "I wanna stay here. With you."

"When you come back tomorrow morning you'll be in my class all day."

"No!" The child spun around and took off at a run.

Surprise made Rachel hesitate. Samantha was already disappearing down an exterior hallway when she came to her senses and started in pursuit.

She didn't dare shout. If Heatherington happened to look out the window and see what was happening she might decide to move Samantha to another class for the short time she had left before being sent out of state. That was the last thing Rachel wanted.

At the corner where the sidewalk made a T, Rachel skidded to a stop. Which way? Left? Right? The hall was deserted.

Breathless, she prayed, "Where is she? Help me? Please, Lord?"

A commotion to the right caught her attention. Though the sounds were muffled, Rachel was certain she heard a childish squeal, followed by a definitely masculine "Oof."

She dashed toward the noise, rounded a blind corner and nearly slammed into the doubled-over figure of Sean Bates! This time, he wasn't laughing.

"Which way?" Rachel demanded.

Breathless, Sean pointed. "What's going on?"

"Tell you later."

"You'd better believe it."

He straightened slowly, painfully, watching Rachel race down the hall in pursuit of the little blond monster that had plowed into him. It had been moving so fast that he wasn't even sure whether it was a girl or a boy. When he saw Rachel returning, holding the child in front of her with its arms and legs thrashing, he still wasn't sure. Not that it mattered.

"Want some help?" he asked.

"Oh, no. I'll just hang on like this until she gets tired. Or until she kills me."

"You don't have to be sarcastic. I said I'd help."

"Sorry. It's been a rough day."

"Tell me about it."

He eyed the red-faced child. Rachel had grabbed her from behind, rendering her kicks useless. If he approached from the front, however, he was liable to be very, very sorry—again.

"I just did tell you," Rachel said. "This is Samantha Smith. She's going to be in my class. I think."

"You sure you want that?" Eyebrows cocked, Sean gave her a lopsided grin.

"Of course I do. Samantha and I just have to come to an understanding first." Rachel raised her voice, speaking slowly, plainly. "If she doesn't decide to settle down and behave pretty soon, I may have to ask Ms. Heatherington to take her to another school. I really don't want to do that."

The little girl gasped, froze in midmotion and stared past Sean's shoulder in the direction of the office. Then she wilted like a plucked blossom on a hot summer day.

Relieved, Rachel relaxed and eased her to the ground so she could stand. "Whew. That's better."

Sean was braced for another escape attempt. It didn't come.

Instead, the girl gazed up at her teacher with new respect. "I— I'm sorry. You won't tell, will you?"

"Not unless I have to. It's my job to keep you safe and teach you how to get along with others. That means you have to listen to me and do as I say. Will you do that from now on?"

The child peered off into the distance one more time, then looked back up at Rachel and nodded solemnly. "Uh-huh."

"Okay. We have a deal."

Rachel held out her hand and Samantha took it. Together, they started to walk back toward the office.

Sean watched them go. He had to admit he'd been wrong to judge the pretty, diminutive teacher on appearance alone. Rachel Woodward was definitely special. One of a kind. Not only was she physically stronger than she looked, she had an indomitable will and a tender, empathetic heart that were impossible to deny.

He smiled to himself. With "credentials" like that, it was no wonder her unconventional form of child psychology had worked so well.

Driving home that evening, Rachel couldn't get memories of Sean Bates out of her mind, so she forced herself to concentrate on her newest student instead. Thinking about Samantha kept her from reliving her recent close encounters with Sean, at least temporarily. She was getting pretty disgusted with herself about that. There was certainly no good reason for her to get the shivers every time she pictured his smile and sparkling eyes.

Rachel was glad she'd paused to examine her innermost thoughts regarding Samantha, because they revealed a truly deep concern. As long as that little girl remained in her class, Rachel knew she'd have to be careful to avoid showing favoritism. All students deserved equal treatment, as much as it was within a teacher's ability to provide it, and getting emotionally attached to one or two individuals made impartiality that much harder.

Rachel pulled into the driveway of her modest, white-painted house. Boy, was she glad to be home. She'd bought the house on Old Sturkie Road at auction and had fixed it up to suit her eclectic taste. Now that she was well settled in, she couldn't imagine ever wanting to move. The place had everything: quaint heritage charm, combined with all the modern conveniences such as running water, indoor plumbing, electricity and telephone. In the winter, Rachel could even supplement her regular heating system by lighting the woodstove that still sat by the chimney in her living room.

In the summer, however, there was nothing she'd rather do than relax in the shade of the covered front porch overlooking her peaceful neighborhood.

The phone was already ringing when she flung open the back door and grabbed the receiver. Between her delay at work and the fact that she'd stopped at the market on the way home to pick up a few things for supper, she was running late. Which meant she had a very good idea who was calling.

"Hi, Mom."

"How'd you know it was me?"

"Lucky guess."

"You didn't call," Martha chided.

"I just walked in the door."

"Hard day?"

"The first ones always are. You know how it is."

"It took you a long time to get home tonight. I've been trying to reach you for over an hour."

Rachel chuckled cynically. "Well, unless you expect Schatzy or Muffin to answer, you'll have to give me time to get here."

Hearing his name, the little black-and-tan dachshund danced at Rachel's feet, circled a couple of times, then ran over to give the lazy, gray angora cat a lick across its face. Muffin showed her displeasure by hissing.

"Stop that," Rachel said.

Confused, Martha asked, "Who? Me?"

"No, not you, Mom. The cat."

"Oh. I never could abide animals in the house, myself. Too messy. All that hair!"

"I keep them brushed. Anyway, Schatzy hardly

sheds.'' Rachel surveyed her homey living room with a contented smile.

"You and your animals."

Here it comes, Rachel thought. She tensed, waiting for her mother to seize the opportunity to point up the difference between keeping pets and raising children.

Instead, Martha said, "I had my hair done today. Mercy Cosgrove was in the beauty shop the same time I was. She says her granddaughter, Emily, is getting married."

"I know."

"Why didn't you tell me?"

"I only found out today. She's marrying Jack Foster."

"Hard to believe, isn't it? I mean, there was a time when she could have had a doctor for a husband. Sam Barryman was ripe for the picking."

"So you've reminded me. Often," Rachel drawled. "Didn't he finally run off and marry Sheila Something-or-other?"

"That's old news," Martha said. "They're getting a divorce."

"Too bad. But it doesn't surprise me. My one date with good old Dr. Sam was enough to cure me—pun intended."

"What about the new guy at your school? I understand he's single. And cute, too."

"News travels fast."

Rachel knew better than to offer additional information about Sean. All she'd have to do was give her mother a hint that she might be interested in him and Martha's wild imagination would take off. Pretty soon, she'd have convinced herself that Rachel was practically engaged to the poor guy, when nothing could be further from the truth.

"Well, have you met him yet?" Martha asked.

"I, uh, I did run into him," Rachel said, laughing to herself and picturing the shocked look on Sean's face when she'd crashed into his broad chest. The vivid memory of his strong hands steadying her followed instantly, leading to an all-over tingle and another little shiver. Maybe she was catching a summer cold or something.

"You wait too long and there won't be any good ones left," Martha said.

"There weren't all that many to start with, Mother."

"I still don't know why you had to break up with that nice Craig Slocum."

Because that nice Craig Slocum dumped me when I told him I might not be able to have kids, Rachel countered silently. She said, "These things happen. Look, Mom, I'm really beat and I have to put my groceries away before they spoil. Can I call you back later?"

"There's no need. I just wanted to hear your voice, to make sure my little girl was okay."

"I'm fine, Mom," Rachel said. "I'm all grown up, remember?"

"You'll always be my little girl, honey."

She laughed lightly. "I can just see us now. I'll be seventy and you'll be ninety-five and you'll still expect me to phone you every day to tell you I'm okay."

"Not a chance," Martha said. "By that time, I'll either be living with you and your family or you'll at least have a husband to look after you so I can quit worrying."

What a choice! Rachel was glad her mother couldn't see the way she was rolling her eyes. "You wouldn't like living in my house, Mom. Animals make you sneeze, remember?"

Martha snickered. "I'll hold my breath. At ninety-five, that shouldn't be hard. It's the breathing in and out part that might get a little tricky."

Rachel wasn't too weary to appreciate her mother's dark humor. "You're amazing."

"You, too, honey. Talk to you tomorrow."

"I'll call you as soon as I get home from work. Don't panic, okay? You know I'm always late when school first starts."

"You shouldn't let them take advantage of you."

"I'm the one who's taking advantage, Mom. I let them pay me for something I'd gladly do for free."

"So, swallow your pride and marry a rich man. Then you can afford to be a volunteer."

"I'd rather eat dirt."

Rachel could hear the smile in her mother's voice when she replied, "I hear dirt is pretty tasty if you pour enough red-eye gravy over it."

Chapter Three

If Samantha had been added to her class after the group had been together longer, Rachel would have made a special point of introducing her. Since it was only the second day of the school year, however, that wouldn't be necessary. Or advisable. The less fuss, the better.

Parents had already escorted many of the other children to the classroom door. It was amusing how often the parent was the one reluctant to let go, while the child was eager to join in the excitement of finally starting school.

Wearing a favorite lightweight summer shirt with a softly draped skirt, Rachel stood in the doorway of her room to welcome her students and gently encourage their parents to leave. She glanced up at the clock on the wall as the final morning bell rang. One child hadn't arrived yet.

A few latecomers rushed by. Concerned, Rachel was about to give up and close the door when she saw a man and a small, blond girl approaching hand-in-hand. It was Samantha!

Rachel's breath caught. Sean Bates was bringing her.

"Thank You, God," she whispered.

Watching their approach she couldn't have said which of the two she was most delighted to see. Each was certainly a welcome sight. And together they made her heart sing.

Unfortunately, the little girl was wearing the same faded T-shirt and baggy blue shorts she'd had on the day before. In contrast to the new school clothes her classmates were sporting, she made a sad figure, indeed. Rachel made a mental note to remedy that situation ASAP. If Heatherington wouldn't see to it that Samantha had proper clothing and shoes for school, she'd do it herself. There was no excuse for sending the little girl out into the world looking like an urchin—even if she was one.

Rachel greeted the latecomers with a broad grin. "Good morning! I'm so glad to see you, Samantha. Did you ride the bus to school?"

Sean spoke up. "I think so. I found her standing out front on the lawn. It looked like she was waiting for directions, so I brought her on over. I hope that's okay."

"Of course. Thank you for helping. We all try to watch out for each other around here." She crouched down to be on the little girl's level and asked again, "Did you ride the bus?"

Samantha nodded.

"Then, it's my fault you had trouble finding my class. I should have shown you how to get here from the place where the buses stop. I'm sorry you had trouble. But I am glad you met Mr. Bates yesterday and that he knew where to bring you."

Instead of paying attention to what Rachel was saying, Samantha gazed up at Sean with evident adoration, then leaned to one side so she could peer at his back.

With a questioning frown, Rachel straightened. Her intense blue gaze wordlessly asked him what was going on.

Sean shrugged, palms out. "That's the third time she's done that." He turned. "Did somebody stick a 'Kick Me' sign on my back when I wasn't paying attention?"

"No. There's nothing there," Rachel assured him. "It's clean." And broad and strong and impressive and… *Oh, stop it,* her conscience demanded, bringing her up short before she had time to give in to the idiotic urge to dust invisible lint off the shoulders of his jacket.

"That's a relief," he said.

Rachel swallowed hard. "Yeah. Well, thanks again for helping Samantha find her class."

"You're quite welcome." He gave a slight bow and grinned at the little girl. "I'll watch tomorrow, too. Okay? After that, I'm sure you'll be able to get here all by yourself.''

"I know she'll be fine." Pausing to give the loitering parents—and Sean—a look that clearly meant she was taking charge, Rachel added, "It's time for class. All the grown-ups have to go, now."

It wasn't until she'd guided Samantha through the door and closed it behind her that she realized her hands were shaking. That third cup of coffee she'd had for breakfast must have provided more caffeine than she'd thought.

To Rachel's relief, the only tears she'd seen that morning had been those of the parents left outside. Some years the opposite was true. Snifflers weren't so bad because they were fairly easy to distract. Screamers were another story. Occasionally, there would be a child who was so afraid of separation from mommy or daddy that hysteria ensued. Not only was the wild sobbing distracting, it tended to spread an unwarranted sense of dread to the others. This year, however, it looked as if the adjustment was going to be peaceful.

Suddenly, an indignant *whoop* disturbed the calm. Children froze and stared. Rachel immediately zeroed in on the cause and hurried to help.

She bent over the screeching little boy. "What's wrong?" *Name—name—what was his name?* And where was the name tag she'd carefully pinned on him when he'd first arrived?

Other children had huddled in small groups, looking on as if expecting dire consequences to spill over onto them.

Rachel guessed. "It's Jimmy, isn't it? What's the matter, Jimmy? Did you hurt yourself? Can you tell me what happened so I can fix it?" By keeping her voice soft she forced the child to quiet down to hear what she was saying.

Jimmy drew a shuddering breath and pointed to a nearby knot of boys. "He hit me."

The knot instantly unraveled as children scattered.

Rachel took charge. "All right. I need everyone to sit down on the rug so we can talk about keeping our hands to ourselves." She pointed. "Jimmy, there's a box of tissues over there. You can go get one and wipe your nose before you come sit with us."

Choosing the adult-size chair at the head of the class, Rachel waited for the children to comply. All but two did. The tearful boy was doing as he'd been told and blowing his nose. Samantha had gone with him.

Rachel was about to remind the little girl that she was a part of the class and needed to behave just like the others, when she noticed something that gave her pause. Although Samantha was whispering to the sniffling boy, her excitement was evident. She waved. She pointed across the room. She held out her arms as if mimicking a bird and smiled so broadly her eyes were squeezed almost shut. Or were they actually closed? Rachel couldn't tell for sure. All she knew was that Jimmy had forgotten about being upset and was giving Samantha his rapt attention.

So, Samantha wanted to play mother. Rachel smiled. That was a good sign. The child obviously needed to feel needed. Looking after the other children would give her a positive purpose, not to mention a boost in morale.

And anybody who can calm a screamer like that is okay in my book, she thought. There was a tender-hearted peacemaker in the class. This was going to be a good year.

A very good year.

The day flew by so fast that it was over before Rachel had time to notice how tired she was. At two-thirty she lined up all her students and marched them out to the lawn in front of the school to make sure each one was handed over to a parent or had boarded the right bus.

Samantha stood by Rachel's side and watched each classmate depart, until only she was left.

"Which bus did you come on?" Rachel asked her, wiping sweat from her own brow and wishing she could escape the sultry southern afternoon by heading back to her air-conditioned classroom.

"I don't know."

"What was the number on it?"

"I don't know." Clearly, the child was about to cry.

"Well, did it have a lady driver or a man?"

"I don't remember."

Terrific. "Okay. Let's go check in the office."

As she turned to lead the way, the little girl gave a happy squeal, shouted, "There! That one," and took off running toward the last bus in line.

Rachel paused, unconvinced. An older child might remember suddenly, but five-year-olds were more likely to remain confused.

She started to follow, then decided to check the office records first. If Samantha had chosen the right bus after all, Rachel didn't want to do anything to undermine her self-confidence. If not, there would be plenty of time to correct the error before the buses pulled out.

She hurried into the office, glad for a temporary respite from the heat and humidity of the September afternoon. "I need to see the Samantha Smith file, Mary." Breezing past the receptionist, she headed straight for the upright filing cabinet.

"I don't think I've finished that one yet. It's probably still here in this pile on my desk." Mary gestured toward a messy stack. "Sorry. We've been swamped. I don't know why so many folks wait till the last minute to register their kids."

"In Samantha's case, I don't think there was a choice. Any idea where her file might be? Top, bottom, middle?" Rachel was already paging through the folders.

"Near the top, I think. Why? Didn't you already see it?"

"Yes, but I don't recall what it said about the foster home placement. She needs to ride a bus and I don't know which one."

"Oops. Maybe we should phone and ask Ms. Heatherington."

"No way. I'd rather spend an hour listening to my mother complain than to have to say two words to that woman."

"She is kind of stuffy. Is that why you dislike her?"

"No. It's her attitude about the children she deals with that makes me mad. She acts like it's their fault that their families fell apart and she got stuck helping them."

"The little Smith girl's an orphan, isn't she?"

"Yes, which makes it even harder. That's why it's so important to be sure she's on the right bus. Life has to be frightening enough for her already."

"Well, you'd better get a move on. It's almost time for those buses to leave."

"I know. I'm hurrying."

Rachel fumbled a file folder and almost dropped it, just as a mother burst through the door and shouted, "There you are. I want to talk to you. Now!"

It took Rachel a moment to realize she was the object of the woman's ire. Her first clue was the small, round-faced boy who was clutching his mother's pudgy finger and rubbing his runny nose with his other hand. It was Jimmy.

"I'll be right with you, Mrs.—"

"Andrews," she said crisply. "My son, James, is in your class, as you well know."

"Yes, ma'am. We can go talk in my room. I just have to take care of—"

"I'm not going anyplace where you can make excuses in private," the woman said. "I want to know, right here and right now, where you get off telling my son that there are *angels* in his classroom?"

"What?" Rachel was totally confused.

"Angels. He says there are guardian angels flying all over the kindergarten room."

"I never told him that."

"Well, somebody sure did."

"Maybe one of the other children." A light went on in Rachel's head. Of course! Samantha hadn't been pretending to be a bird when she'd comforted Jimmy, she'd been demonstrating her ideas about angels! *How sweet.*

Rachel nodded, convinced of her conclusions. "I think I know what happened to confuse your son. Children have wonderful imaginations. One of the girls must have told him about angels this morning while she was helping him blow his nose."

Mrs. Andrews wasn't placated. "Well, what if she did? You're the teacher. What are you going to do about it?"

"Nothing. No harm's been done," she said calmly. "Now, if you'll excuse me, I have to go hold the buses until I can be sure one of my students is on the right one."

"Well! I never…"

The woman was still muttering to herself when Rachel brushed past and headed for the curb. Her eyes widened in disbelief.

The buses were already gone!

After a hurried search of the hallways and her own classroom, Rachel returned to the office, gave in and telephoned Heatherington's office.

When she hung up, Mary asked, "Well?"

"Samantha's living with the Brodys on Squirrel Hill Road. I saw her get on bus number seven. I think she belonged on five." Rachel began pacing. "It's my fault. I should have kept her with me until I knew for sure."

"She'll be okay. Surely, the driver will notice and… Oh-oh. Seven, did you say?"

"Yes. Why?"

"Because we have a sub driving that one this afternoon."

"Don't tell me. Let me guess. Sean Bates is driving seven, right?"

"No, Maxwell Eades is." Mary frowned. "Why would you think it was Sean Bates?"

"Because Samantha knows Sean. I figured she'd choose that bus if she saw him behind the wheel."

"Nope. Sorry. We can't use Bates until he gets an Arkansas license. Mr. Vanbruger did suggest he ride along to familiarize himself with the routes, though. He could have decided to start with any of them."

"Give me maps of all the routes," Rachel ordered. "Then please get on the phone and alert some of the parents who live along seven. Ask them to tell Max to keep Samantha from getting off."

Mary handed her copies of hand-drawn maps. "Gotcha. What are you going to do?"

"Jump in my car and try to catch the bus before that poor kid gets herself totally lost."

"Isn't that above and beyond the call of duty?"

"Not for me it isn't. And definitely not where Samantha Smith is concerned. The minute I saw her I knew I was meant to look after her. So far I haven't done a very good job of it. From now on, I intend to do a lot better."

Rachel was familiar with the rural area where the Brody family lived, but since Samantha's bus wasn't headed that way, the knowledge was no help. The only sensible thing to do was trace the bus route, mile by mile, until she overtook number seven.

And what if Samantha's already gotten off before I catch up to her? Rachel's heart sped. *Or what if she changed buses at school while I was stuck in the office?*

Stomach in knots, Rachel tightened her grip on the wheel of her compact car, sweating in spite of the air-conditioning. She mustn't think such negative thoughts. They only made everything seem worse.

Prayer would be a much better choice, yet she was unable to force her worried mind to concentrate enough to come up with a lucid plea. Finally, she resorted to a misty-eyed *Please, God,* and left it at that.

She made good time until she turned off the highway onto the narrow, winding road that ran between Glencoe and Heart. According to old-timers, Heart had once been a thriving little town. It had even had its own post office inside a mom-and-pop grocery store. For decades, that had been a favorite local gathering place, especially on Friday nights when weekly paychecks needed to be cashed. Now, however, Heart consisted of a couple of isolated houses and a community center building that was used mainly on Wednesdays by a quilting club.

This was Tuesday. If Samantha got off the school bus in Heart, she wouldn't meet a soul who could help her.

Rachel chewed on her lower lip. "Calm down. Stop imagining the worst. You'll find her."

Head spinning, thoughts churning, Rachel pictured possible scenarios. If Samantha truly had boarded that particular bus because Sean was on it, she'd want to stay near him. She wouldn't be likely to get off at all! Then again, if she hadn't...

The pavement ended abruptly. Rachel slowed and pulled over in front of the Heart Community Center to double-check her map. She frowned. She'd seen kindergartners draw clearer diagrams.

The building sat in a rocky, dusty triangle at the confluence of the roads. One track was supposed to lead to Saddle, one to Salem with a cutoff to Camp, and the other to Agnos. Bus seven should be headed for Camp, which meant the first thing she needed to find was the branch of the road that led toward Salem.

She peered west. *That one.* It had to be that one. She could see the red lights flashing on the radio station antennae atop the hill called the Salem Knob.

Decision made, Rachel tromped the accelerator. Her car's wheels spun in the loose gravel and dirt, leaving behind a cloud of powdery red dust. It was a blessing that Max was driving the bus, because he knew where he was going. She'd lived around here all her life and she still sometimes got turned around when she left the highway. An inexperienced person like Sean, using the same map she'd been given, would be likely to get lost.

Seeing more dust ahead was encouraging. Rachel cautiously increased her speed. She didn't want to go too fast. The roads had recently been scraped by county graders, making the center smoother but uncovering and scattering enough sharp rocks to make driving more hazardous than usual. Previous vehicles had left tracks in passing; Rachel tried to keep her tires in those same ruts to avoid unnecessary risk.

Rounding a corner she came upon a sight that made her heart pound. Bus seven! Now, all she had to do was get it to pull over so she could be certain Samantha was still safely aboard.

Approaching the slow-moving bus she flashed her lights and honked. Small faces peered out the bus's

rear windows at her, grinning and waving. She sig-
naled as best she could, but the children apparently
thought she was merely being friendly because they
returned her greeting with renewed vigor.

According to the map, it was miles before the next
bus stop. Rachel was too frustrated to wait that long
to learn Samantha's fate, yet it was unsafe to pass the
lumbering bus on such a treacherous road.

"Give me patience, Lord, and hurry," she muttered, laughing at the contradiction. *God is in charge,
God is in charge,* she reminded herself.

Finally, she laid on the horn and held it. That
worked. Max pulled the bus over. Rachel stopped behind it, jumped out and was immediately enveloped
in a noxious cloud of exhaust fumes and unsettled
dust.

Ignoring the discomfort, she forged ahead, waving
her arms wildly, and circled to the front of the bus.
Max had already opened the folding doors.

Sean was standing on the top step, steadying himself by holding on to a chrome support pole. He
wasn't smiling. "Are you nuts?"

"Yes." Rachel coughed as she boarded and pushed
him aside. "Where's Samantha?"

"Right there." He pointed. "Mind telling me
what's going on? Or do you always drive like a ma-
niac?"

Aside from being choked up by the fumes, Rachel
was also dizzy and breathless with relief. She wa-
vered, then plunked down next to Samantha, speaking

to the wide-eyed child. "I was so worried. This isn't your bus, honey. It won't take you to Mrs. Brody's."

The little girl's eyes grew moist. She blinked. "Oh."

Sean made himself part of their conversation and addressed Rachel. "Then, why did you let her get on it in the first place?"

She raised her gaze, her expression a clear challenge. "I made a mistake, okay? I know that now. I thought I'd be… Oh, never mind." Getting to her feet she reached for the little girl's hand. "Come on, honey. I'll take you home."

Sean blocked her path. "Over my dead body. You're far too agitated to drive. The way you were acting just now you shouldn't even have been behind the wheel of a car, let alone consider transporting kids."

"I beg your pardon."

Facing him, Rachel stood as tall as her short stature would permit and tried to appear formidable. Pitted against his broad chest and wide stance, her effort seemed more pitiful than confrontational. He'd removed his jacket and tie and rolled up the sleeves of his dress shirt. If anything, that made him look even more rugged, more powerful than usual.

"You should beg everybody's pardon, lady."

Before Rachel could reply, Max cut in. "Save your breath, folks. Miz Rachel ain't goin' nowhere. Looks like she's gettin' herself a dandy flat tire." He leaned to the left to get a better look at her car in his rearview mirror.

"That's impossible," she insisted. "I was very careful. And I wasn't speeding."

"Out here it don't matter much," Max said. "You'd best go check before I head on down the road with these here kids. It's a mighty long walk to town."

"Oh, for heaven's sake." She edged past Sean and hurried back to inspect her car. It was definitely listing to one side. Her shoulders slumped. "Oh, no."

Sean had quietly followed. "I'd help you change that tire," he said, "but unless you carry two spares, we'd still be one short."

"What?"

He pointed at one of the rear wheels. "Looks to me like you've got a second tire going flat."

Thunderstruck, Rachel realized he could be right. Her eyes widened. "I don't believe this!"

"I do. I may be from the city but even I know better than to go racing around on rocky roads like these."

"I wasn't racing!" Disgusted with everyone and everything, she let it show in her expression.

"Tell that to your car," Sean said.

"Okay, okay. You don't have to rub it in." Pausing, she considered her current options. "I suppose I could walk to the nearest house and call a garage."

"You could. Or, you could just leave your car where it sits and ride back to school on the bus with us. That way, you and I could take Samantha home in my car, then I could drive you back here afterward.''

''What good will that do if there's more than one ruined tire?''

''Simple. We'll take them off, load them in my trunk and find a garage that'll patch them.''

Rachel was astounded. ''You'd do that for me?''

''No problem. I'm glad to help—as long as I don't have to *ride* with you,'' Sean chided, ignoring the face she was making at him. ''I don't think I'm that brave.'' He chuckled softly, enjoying her discomfiture. ''I don't think *anybody* is.''

Chapter Four

By the time Max had dropped off his last regular passengers and returned to Serenity Elementary, it was nearly five p.m. There were only two cars in the parking lot—Sean's black sedan and a silver-colored, dusty van.

Rachel led Samantha up the front walk toward the school office as she spoke over her shoulder to Sean. "Before we go, I need to phone Mrs. Brody so she knows everything is all right."

"I don't think that'll be necessary," he said, gesturing. "We've never met, but I'd say she's just found us."

Oh dear. He was right. She was about to face *another* irate grown-up. Hannah Brody had thrown open the door of the van and was shuffling rapidly across the parking lot, shirttail flapping, bangs glued to her forehead with perspiration. Rachel had never seen the poor woman look more frazzled.

"Hannah! I'm sorry if we worried you," Rachel shouted before she reached them. "Samantha accidentally got on the wrong bus. I was just bringing her back."

"You couldn't *call* me? Let me know?" The older, slightly portly woman wheezed to a stop as she confronted Rachel. "Do you know how hot it got in that there van? I coulda croaked, waitin' on y'all."

"I'm really sorry," Rachel said. "I was worried, too. Guess I wasn't thinking clearly."

Hannah leaned down to focus on the child. "And you. How old are you?"

"F-five."

"So, how did we say you could remember the number of your bus?"

The child stared at the toes of her worn sneakers. "Five. Same as me."

"That's right."

"What a good idea," Rachel interjected, trying to sound upbeat.

Hannah straightened and glared at her, hands fisted on ample hips. "Now you, missy. What do you have to say for yourself?"

"Excuse me?"

"There is no excuse for what you did."

Sean stepped up beside Rachel, clearly taking sides. "Most teachers would probably have left the child's welfare in the hands of the bus driver. Ms. Woodward, however, took it upon herself to try to put things right. That speaks very well for her, don't you agree?''

For the first time, Hannah took notice of Sean. She gave him a critical once-over. ''And who might you be?''

He introduced himself and extended a hand of friendship. The annoyed woman begrudgingly accepted it. Then, instead of stuffing his hands into his pockets the way he initially had when he'd run into the pretty teacher in the hallway, he took half a step closer to Rachel and nonchalantly looped one arm around her shoulders. The gesture was casual yet obviously protective.

Mrs. Brody noticed immediately. Her eyebrows arched. ''Oh, I see. You two were too busy playing patty-cake to pay attention to anything else.'' She grabbed the child's hand and started away. ''Well, what's done is done. Come on, Samantha. It's too late to take you shopping for new clothes today like I'd promised. I got to go start supper.''

The little girl glanced back over her shoulder, silently pleading with her teacher and Sean to rescue her as Hannah Brody led her away. That soulful look was enough to put Rachel's heart in a twist and leave a lump in her throat.

For an instant she wanted to weep. Instead, she

waved, smiled and called, "Bye-bye. See you tomorrow, Samantha."

"Will she be okay with that old grump?" Sean asked softly.

"Hannah?" Rachel glanced up at him while deliberately removing his hand from her shoulder. "Hannah's not a bad person. She gets a little irritable sometimes but she's basically good-hearted. She's been taking in the kids nobody else wanted to bother with for years."

"Samantha's one of those?"

"Apparently. Her social worker did say she was having trouble adjusting. That's probably why they gave her to Hannah."

"I see. What else can you tell me about the Brody woman?"

"Well…" Rachel's smile stayed. "She baby-sat for lots of folks here in Serenity who're all grown up, now. Me included."

"You're kidding! No wonder you let her talk to you like that."

"Hannah means well. And she was right. I should have called her so she wouldn't worry. I was so worried about finding Samantha, I guess it just slipped my mind."

"That's understandable. Don't beat yourself up about it."

"I won't. The only thing that bothers me is the way

the small-town rumor mill is going to have fun with us.''

"Us?" Sean's expression showed bewilderment. "What *us?*"

With a wry chuckle, Rachel shook her head. "You do have a lot to learn about living in a place like this, don't you. There doesn't even have to be an *us* for people to talk. By tomorrow morning, half the folks in town will be saying you and I are practically engaged. And the other half will be trying to decide if you're good enough for me."

She'd expected Sean to enjoy the lighthearted banter. Instead, he seemed upset. She pressed on. "Hey, don't look so glum. I didn't say it was my idea. It's just how it is in a place where everybody knows everybody else, and half of them are related, besides." That statement brought a further conclusion. "Oh-oh."

"What's wrong now?"

"I just had a horrible thought. Hannah's my mother's second cousin by marriage."

"So?"

"So, I'll bet Mom is the first one she calls."

Sean huffed. "Don't tell me you're still worried about pleasing your mother at your age?"

"Hey. I'm not *that* old."

He deliberately took his time looking her up and down and fully appreciating what he saw. Chances were good that he was at least seven or eight years older than she was, maybe more, yet they had to be contemporaries in spite of her youthful appearance. For starters, he knew this wasn't Rachel's first year of teaching. A person didn't usually finish college and earn a degree until they were in their twenties at least, so she had to be halfway to thirty by now.

"You don't look a day over sixteen," he finally told her.

"Actually, I'll be eighty-four my next birthday," she said. Struggling to repress a giggle, she twirled in a circle to put herself on display. "Pretty good for an octogenarian, huh?"

"Excellent." Sean was shaking his head in disbelief and laughing softly under his breath. "You certainly had me fooled. What's your secret?"

"Clean living. I never miss a Sunday in church, either."

"Very commendable."

"I think so. Hey! Since you're new in town, how'd you like to come visit my church?"

"Church and I don't exactly get along."

"That's too bad. We won't eat you, you know. We really do accept everybody, even *sinners.*" The astonishment in his expression made her chuckle. "That was a joke, Bates."

"I'll laugh later, okay?" He reached into his pocket for his car keys and jingled them in one hand. "You ready?"

"As soon as I go grab my purse," Rachel said. "Wait here. I'll just be a minute."

Starting away she heard him mutter, "I don't believe it."

She spun around. "You don't believe what?"

"You. You were driving all over the country without your license?"

"Guess I was. I told you Christians aren't perfect. You'd better start believing me or I may have to keep trying to prove it to you."

Rachel's car was right where she'd left it, without so much as a hubcap missing—much to Sean's surprise. A prankster had scrawled "Wash me" and drawn a happy face in the fresh layer of dust coating the lid of the trunk, but otherwise the car was untouched.

He parked as far off the roadway as he could without scratching his sedan on the brambles and small trees growing along the right-of-way, and got out. Rachel followed.

A closer look at her car made her sigh audibly. Her shoulders sagged. "Rats. You were right. I do have two flats."

"Apparently." Sean circled the car, assessing the damage. "Looks to me as if it's going to be dangerous to remove the tires, even if we use both our jacks. The ground is too uneven here. The car wouldn't be stable."

"What do you suggest, then?"

"Calling a tow truck. If we left your car jacked up and drove into town with two of the wheels, any little thing could knock it over and damage the axles. Then we'd have to call a tow, anyway."

Rachel was too exhausted to argue. She yawned. "Fine. Whatever. As long as I can get to work in the morning."

"I don't suppose you happen to know the number of a local garage that does towing?" he asked, reaching into his car for his cellular phone and pushing the power button.

She snorted cynically. "As a matter of fact, I do."

Sean waited, growing impatient when she didn't recite the number. "Well?"

"It wouldn't be my first choice."

"This is not a popularity contest. If this place can come get your car and fix the tires, let's get on with it, okay?"

"Okay, okay."

Rachel gave him the number, then watched as he made arrangements with the garage. To her surprise, Sean knew approximately where they were and gave credible directions, so she didn't have to interrupt to correct him.

That was a plus. So was the lengthening day. If Craig Slocum had already gone home for supper, as she hoped, her personal involvement could be kept to a minimum.

And if not? She clenched her jaw, imagining Craig's superior smirk when he discovered she needed his help. Since their failed engagement, Rachel had managed to avoid him almost completely. If he showed up this evening it would be the first time she'd spoken to him face-to-face since he broke her heart.

Her chin jutted out, her spine stiffened. If she had to face Craig, she would meet the challenge head-on. That man was never going to learn how deeply he had hurt her. *Never.*

Sean noticed Rachel's growing uneasiness. When they heard the approach of a truck, her head snapped around and she stared in the direction of the sound as if expecting a stalking tiger instead of deliverance.

"Want to tell me why you're so jumpy?" he asked.

"I'm not jumpy."

There was nothing to be gained by arguing with her. "Okay. Sorry." Sean smiled. "Maybe you're just hungry. Personally, I'm starved. What do you say we grab a pizza or something while we wait for your car to be fixed?"

Rachel nodded without taking her eyes off the distant roadway as the truck rumbled closer.

Sean decided to test her. "Your treat."

"Sure. Fine."

His resultant laugh finally got Rachel's attention. She frowned. "What's so funny?"

"You are. I could have asked you anything just now and you'd have agreed without hearing a word I said."

"Don't be silly."

"Okay. We are on for dinner, then?"

"Dinner? Oh, sure. Only around here, dinner is what we eat at lunchtime. The evening meal is called supper."

"I'll remember that." He saw the tow truck slowing. Inside the cab, its driver was grinning from ear to ear. The man's eyes were shadowed by the brim of his baseball cap, but it was still evident he was concentrating on Rachel.

"You know him?" Sean asked.

"I told you. Everybody knows everybody around here."

"Let me put it another way," Sean said quietly. "Do you dislike him as much as I think you do?"

She huffed and managed a momentary smile. "Actually, Craig and I used to be engaged."

"Engaged? You were going to marry *him?*"

"Yes." Her frown returned. "Why is that so surprising?"

"I don't know. I guess he just doesn't look like your type."

"Why not? Because he drives a tow truck?" The Slocums owned several lucrative businesses in Serenity and the surrounding area, and Craig drove the tow rig because he liked to, but Rachel wasn't about to explain all that to Sean.

"Listen, Mr. Bates," she said firmly, "if a man does an honest job and is proud of his work, I see no reason to put him down simply because he may not have a college degree like you and I do. If you choose your friends by their level of formal education, you'll miss out on a whole lot, especially around here. There are plenty of very smart folks who haven't had the opportunities you and I have had."

Sean was grinning at her. "You through?"

"I just don't like stuck-up people, that's all."

"Neither do I." He chuckled softly, shook his head. "I was talking about the smug, know-it-all look on the guy's face. I didn't think you'd put up with that kind of attitude for a second. Since you two broke up, apparently I was right."

Chagrined, she wished she hadn't jumped to conclusions. "Sorry about the lecture. Class distinction is a sore point with me."

"So I've gathered." Sean was still grinning. "Well, here comes your ex-fiancé. Mind if I shake hands with him?"

"Of course not."

"Good." He stepped forward, his hand extended. "I'm Sean Bates. Thanks for coming so promptly. We really appreciate it."

The other man paused to glance at Rachel, then

turned back to Sean and gave his hand a pump. "Craig Slocum."

His grip was more than firm, it was crushing. If Sean hadn't known the man's history with Rachel and anticipated the animosity, he would have been taken aback by the overt show of strength. Instead, he met it equally.

"We aim to please," Craig said. "What seems to be the problem here?"

"A pair of flats," Sean answered. "Like I told your dispatcher, we can't safely repair the damage as the car sits. Think you can load it up on your truck and get it back to town for us? Ms. Woodward needs her car in time for work tomorrow."

Craig pushed his cap back on his head and wiped his brow with a red-printed kerchief as he studied the dusty car. Rachel, on the other hand, looked at her feet, at the tree-dotted farmland all around them, at the peacefully grazing cows with their new calves—everywhere except at her former fiancé.

Interested, Sean watched the unspoken interplay between the two. It seemed to him that a spark of romance remained. Then again, he could be imagining things.

Tension hung in the sultry air, blurring the truth like fog on a dewy morning. Slocum wasn't a big man but he was definitely physically fit, Sean noted, which probably appealed to Rachel, at least on a subconscious level. They had undoubtedly made a good-looking couple. Perhaps they would again.

As soon as Craig had winched Rachel's car onto the flatbed of his truck and secured it with heavy chains, he opened the passenger door of the wrecker and flashed her a killer smile. "Ready, hon?"

The expression of panic in her eyes spurred Sean to answer, "We're ready." Taking Rachel's arm, he escorted her to his car and politely held the door for her, behaving as if there was no question who would drive her back to town.

Sean could feel the other man's angry stare. What had he gotten himself into? In town less than a week and already he'd run afoul of one of the good ole boys whose unofficial buddy system ran everything inside and outside of Serenity. These might not be the days of the Hatfields and the McCoys, but Sean knew it wasn't smart to alienate the natives, either. No telling whose uncle or cousin would show up on the school board and wind up voting not to continue funding the counseling program next year. Even a born-and-bred city boy knew that much.

He climbed in beside Rachel and started the car. "You okay?"

"Of course. Why wouldn't I be?"

"No special reason. If you'd explained why you didn't want to call that particular garage, we could have done things differently, you know."

"Slocum's is the best and the fastest. It made sense to use them."

"Not if running into Craig was going to bother you."

"The problem is mine, not his."

"You're the one who broke up with him, then?"

"Not exactly. It was mutual."

Puzzled, Sean glanced over at her as he slowly followed the tow truck, keeping his distance so he wouldn't get a rock chip in his windshield. "Then, why do you say the problem is yours?"

She pulled a face and quickly looked away, embarrassed to admit, even to herself, that she hadn't been able to forgive her former fiancé the way the scripture taught.

Staring out at the passing countryside she said, "Because he's over it and I'm not."

Chapter Five

The drive back to Serenity ended sooner than Sean wanted it to. Rachel had said very little more after her telling comment about her failed relationship with Craig Slocum, and there was no way Sean could hope to help her cope unless she chose to open up to him. Then again, she hadn't asked for that kind of help, had she. So why did he feel compelled to give it? *Good question. Why, indeed?*

Because I'm a "fixer" at heart, he told himself. *Always have been, always will be.*

Though he'd failed to help his own family, that didn't mean he couldn't help others, like Rachel—or the children he'd been trained to work with. That way, at least something good would come out of his troubled childhood. Such assurances gave him solace when he was foolish enough to think back on the trauma of having been raised in a household where he was the only one who wasn't a problem drinker.

Sean parked in front of the service station garage and started to get out. "I'll be right back. I just want to tell Slocum where we're going and when to expect us back." He grinned. "Uh, where are we going and when will we be back?"

"I'm not sure. There won't be any real restaurants open tonight. I suppose we'll have to settle for Hickory Station if we want to eat this late. We passed it on the way in. It's not much to look at but the food's pretty good."

Frowning, Sean glanced at his wristwatch. "What do you mean restaurants won't be open? It's not even seven yet."

"No, but it is Tuesday." Rachel had to laugh at his obvious puzzlement. "This place isn't like Little Rock. Or Cleveland either, I imagine. Folks around here seldom eat out in the evening except on Friday and Saturday nights, so those are the only nights most restaurants stay open past late afternoon."

"You're kidding!"

"Not at all. Breakfast and lunch are different, of course, because people are out and about then. By evening, everyone is home relaxing and getting chores done. We don't stay up late in the country." She smiled broadly, her vivid blue eyes twinkling. "And we don't waste money eating out unless it's payday or we're celebrating the weekend."

"A guy could starve to death around here."

"Unless he had a local guide like me." Rachel peered out at where Craig was unloading her flat-footed car. "Tell him we'll be back in about an hour. There's no need to be more specific. Nobody ever is."

"Kind of puts a whole new spin on the word *casual*," Sean said with a lopsided grin. "Okay. Hang loose. I'll be right back."

Rachel watched him jog away from her. He was good-looking all right, but awfully restrained for a knight in shining armor. The poor guy was totally out of his element in a place like Serenity. He was game, though. And he had a decent sense of humor. That would probably carry him through, as long as he didn't make too many local enemies right off the bat. Country folk were some of the most loving people there were, yet they also remembered every slight, every error in judgment. It didn't take much to alienate a whole community.

"Guess it's up to me to shepherd him until he gets the hang of things," Rachel murmured to herself. "Humph. Just what I need. Another people project." The thought made her smile.

Sean climbed back into the car. "All set." He paused to glance at her. "You look pleased with yourself. What's up?"

"Nothing. I was just thinking."

"About good old Craig?"

The smile vanished. "Don't be silly."

Busying himself backing out and turning the car around, Sean avoided making eye contact with her. "Hey, you don't have to keep up appearances for my sake. I'm neutral, remember? Think of me as your shrink. Anything you want to tell me will remain privileged information. If you're interested in making up with him, I'll be glad to help." Sean was warming to his subject. "You know, give you pointers from the male point of view, stuff like that."

Stunned, Rachel stared over at him. "Let me get this straight. Are you offering advice on my love life?"

"One professional to another. No charge."

"That's big of you." She folded her arms across her chest and stared straight ahead. "You're starting to sound just like my mother. What makes you think I can't handle my own problems?"

"I never said you couldn't. I like to see folks happy, that's all."

"I assure you, Mr. Bates, I'm as happy as a kid in a candy store." Her voice rose. "As a bee in a rose garden. As a hound dog baying at a full moon. As…"

"Okay, okay, I get the idea. You forgot 'Happy as a pig in a mud hole.'"

"I skipped that one on purpose." Making a face at him Rachel felt the beginnings of another smile twitching at the corners of her mouth. "I was trying to keep my analogies from getting too earthy."

"So, you do care what others think of you."

"Of course I do."

"Good. In that case, I should mention that your former boyfriend threatened me back there."

"No way. Craig doesn't care what I do or who I'm with."

"I wouldn't be so sure about that. He told me that if I didn't treat you right, he was going to break every bone in my body." Sean grinned over at her. "Sounds to me like he still cares for you. Either that or he took an instant dislike to me for no reason."

"That's ridiculous."

"If you say so. Nevertheless, the guy looks like he could bench-press a bus axle, so I'd appreciate it if you didn't complain about me in front of him. I value these bones."

And nice bones they are, Rachel thought, eyeing him surreptitiously. Considering how good-looking and appealing Sean was, it wasn't hard to imagine that Craig had been jealous. Even if he didn't want her for himself anymore, she supposed he wouldn't want to see her interested in an outsider.

"I still think you're overreacting, but I'll talk to Craig when we pick up my car and make sure you don't have anything to worry about." Rachel pointed out the car window as a busy quick-stop came into view. "There's Hickory Station. The red-and-white building on the right. Pull in anywhere. We'll go inside to eat."

"It's a gas station."

"Among other things." Rachel had to laugh at him. "You'd better get used to not having candlelit dining rooms, linen tablecloths and highbrow waiters, Bates. This is rural Arkansas, not some metropolis."

She led the way to the door and stepped aside so Sean could open it for her. Thankfully, he had that part of Southern manners down pat.

Tantalizing aromas immediately caught and held her attention. The front cash register was located at the end of a deli counter where fried chicken, potatoes and corn dogs stood in trays under heat lamps. Beyond that array was a pizza oven, and a separate service area with tables and benches for those who wanted to eat there instead of taking their food home.

Rachel recognized one of the cashiers as a young woman she'd gone to school with but had never gotten to know well. The two employees manning the kitchen were older members of her church. Fortunately, no one else with close personal connections to her was present, which helped her relax.

"I'm going to go get myself a soda," she told Sean. "Want me to get one for you, too?"

"Sure. Anything." He was gravitating toward the enticing aroma of freshly baking pizza. "What would you like to eat?"

"Food. Surprise me. I'm hungry enough to eat cardboard."

"Me, too."

By the time Rachel brought their drinks to a table,

he was waiting for her. She slid into the opposite side of the booth, taking care to gather up the extra folds of her skirt and tuck them neatly beside her.

"They were all out of plain cardboard, so I ordered a deluxe special," Sean said. "Hope that's okay."

"It's wonderful." Sighing, Rachel took a deep draft of her icy soda. "I didn't know how tired I was until now. Guess I've been running on adrenaline."

"Me, too."

Weary, she let down her guard enough to reach over and pat the back of his hand where it rested on the table. "Thanks for all you've done for me. I really am grateful."

He froze, glanced at her hand atop his, then withdrew from her touch with a terse "You're welcome."

Rachel giggled. "Hey, I wasn't making a pass at you."

"I never said you were."

"No, but you acted like it."

"I did not."

"Did so."

"Did not." His eyes narrowed. "You're the one who warned me about the local gossip mill. It's going to be pretty hard to convince anybody we're not involved if word gets around that we were holding hands over a pizza."

"Okay. You've made your point," Rachel said. She settled back against the hard plastic of the booth.

"For the record, I want you to know I'm not looking for romance—or anything like that."

"Glad to hear it. Neither am I."

That piqued her curiosity. "Any particular reason?"

"Many. All good."

"And private, I suppose."

"Very."

She began to smile over at him. "You don't mind quizzing me about *my* love life, though, do you."

"That's different."

"Oh? In what way?"

"Because I'm in a position to help you if you'll let me."

"And I suppose I'm not smart enough to do the same for you?"

Sean snorted derisively. "You do have a way of twisting whatever I say, don't you. All I meant was—"

"I know exactly what you meant," Rachel countered. "You have the degree in psychology and you come from a cosmopolitan background, so naturally you're much more enlightened than a simple country girl like me."

She tossed her head, swinging her hair back over her shoulders, her chin jutting out proudly. "Don't make the mistake of selling us country folk short, Mr. Bates. We may not be as sophisticated or as professionally educated as some people you've met, but we're not stupid. I'd lots rather be stranded on a desert island with an Arkansas hillbilly than with a college professor.''

Sean chuckled. ''Are you through?''

''Yes.'' Folding her arms across her chest she faced him boldly, defiantly.

''Good. Then, just sit there. I'm going to see if dinner's ready. Okay?''

Rachel pulled a face and said, ''Not dinner. *Supper.*''

She watched Sean shake his head and laugh softly to himself all the way to the counter. When he turned around with the pizza tray in his hands his amusement was so evident that it brightened his whole face.

In retrospect, Rachel didn't know how she'd managed to get through the remainder of the long day. By the time she and Sean had reclaimed her car and she'd driven home, she was so exhausted she'd simply fed her hungry pets, showered and gone straight to bed. Even the knots of tension in her shoulders and neck hadn't kept her from sleep.

By morning she felt almost human again, which was a good thing, since she had another full day ahead of her.

She'd decided on a simple skirt and blouse and was rummaging through her small closet, looking for matching sandals, when the telephone rang. That was when she noticed the blinking red light on her answering machine. She knew who had called—and who was on the line this time.

"Hi, Mom."

Martha Woodward didn't bother with a greeting. "Where *were* you?"

"It's a long story."

"So I heard. What was wrong with your car?"

Rachel sighed. If her mother knew that much, she knew the rest of the story. "Flat tires."

"I heard that, too. I'm glad you called Craig. He's such a nice boy."

"I called the tow truck, Mother. Craig just happened to be driving it." *Good thing he wasn't there when we went back to get my car.*

"The Lord works in mysterious ways," Martha said.

"I hardly think God assigned Craig to tow truck duty last night just so he could look after me."

"Why not? Stranger things have happened. Besides, I understand you needed rescuing. Who better to do it than the man you were planning to marry?" She sighed wistfully. "You two make such a lovely couple."

"*Made.* Past tense, Mom. I'm never going to be a Slocum, so you might as well give it up."

"If you weren't so stubborn, I'm sure you and Craig could work out your differences."

Boy, am I glad I didn't tell her everything, Rachel

mused. *I'd never hear the end of it.* "That's between Craig and me, Mom. I don't want to discuss it."

"I know, I know. Which reminds me, I talked to cousin Hannah yesterday. Who's the new man at your school? She says he drives the bus."

"He's just a guy. Nobody special."

"That's good, dear. I'd hate for you to get a reputation for taking up with any man who paid you mind. Especially since you and Craig broke up so suddenly."

"Mother…"

"Okay. I'll try to quit worrying. But you'll always be my little girl, no matter how old you get. You know that."

"So you've said. Listen, if I don't get a move on I'm going to be late for work. As it is, I'll be lucky to have time to grab a bite of breakfast."

"Too bad you didn't bring home the leftovers last night," Martha drawled. "You used to love cold pizza for breakfast. Bye, dear. Have a nice day."

To Rachel's delight, Samantha arrived wearing new, clean clothes. Hannah Brody delivered her to the classroom door and stepped inside to make sure the child was okay.

As soon as Rachel had greeted the little girl she turned to Hannah. "Thanks for seeing that she made it."

The older woman made a sour face. "It was my

fault yesterday. I'm sorry. My diabetes had kicked up that morning and I felt like a limp dishrag, so I sent her on the bus. She's a bright little thing. I never dreamt she'd get herself all turned around like that.''

''We all made mistakes,'' Rachel said kindly. ''How are you feeling today?''

''Much better, thanks.'' She swiped at her damp brow. ''It's gonna be another hot one, though.''

''I know. I've been leaving the air conditioner on at home so my poor animals don't cook while I'm gone.''

''You still got that cute little wiener dog?''

''Schatzy? Yes. It's been two years since I brought him home, and Muffin is still sulking. I don't think she'll ever get over having a dog living under the same roof.''

''Reminds me of some of the kids I've looked after over the years.'' Hannah glanced toward Samantha. ''This one's sweeter than most, but she's got some strange ideas, that's a fact.''

''Oh? Like what?'' Stepping closer for privacy Rachel cocked an ear toward the veteran foster mother. Hannah's instincts had been honed over the years and whatever observations she made were bound to be useful.

''She sees things that ain't there,'' the older woman whispered. ''I can't tell whether she's just got a good imagination or if she really believes it.''

''Like what?''

"She says she can see guardian angels."

Angels? Again? "I know," Rachel said. "She told one of the other kids there were angels in the classroom. His mother got mad at me because she thought I was teaching spiritual ideology. Anything else?"

"Not that I know of. She's only been at my place for a few days. If I figure out any more, I'll let you know."

"I appreciate that. And if I learn anything that I think will help you, I'll do the same."

Hannah patted Rachel on the shoulder. "You're a good girl. I knew from the time you was little you'd make a wonderful teacher. Always readin' to the other kids and makin' sure they could write their names. Like it came natural to you."

"I guess it did." She surveyed her busy classroom with a blissful smile. "There's nothing I'd rather do. No place I'd rather be than here."

"I can tell. Well, I'd best be goin'. Now that I know what size our little darlin' wears, I can pick her up a few new outfits on my way home. Just happened to have that blue one she's wearin' in a box of extra clothes. I try to keep nice things on hand. You never know when a new kid'll show up or how long they'll stay, and I can't always get out to go shopping." She chuckled under her breath. "Had to throw those old shorts of hers into the wash machine to get her to stop wearin' 'em. She said her mama gave 'em to her. I didn't think I was ever goin' to get her out of 'em. Not even to sleep.''

"Well, one step at a time," Rachel said as Hannah started for the door. "Will you be coming to get her this afternoon, or shall I put her on the bus?"

The older woman held up one hand, fingers splayed. "The bus. Number *five*."

Laughing, Rachel nodded. "I don't think I'll ever forget that. I imagine I'll be having flashbacks about yesterday afternoon for years to come!"

Hannah paused at the open door and gestured with a jerk of her head. "Speak of the devil. Look who's here."

It wasn't necessary for Rachel to be told that Sean was nearby. Her thudding pulse had informed her of his presence the moment she'd heard him call a greeting to someone else on the playground. That, coupled with the judgmental expression on Hannah's face, was plenty of forewarning.

"He works here," Rachel alibied, fighting to keep her tone even. "I'd expect him to be on campus."

"More's the pity. Well, take care. Tell your mama hello for me when you see her, y'hear."

"Of course."

Though Rachel was bidding the foster mother goodbye, her attention was riveted on Sean. He seemed especially chipper today. There was a spring in his step, a twinkle in his eyes. He looked happy. Too happy. It was disconcerting.

When he got closer and his focus narrowed on Rachel, she chanced a cautious smile. "Good morning."

"It certainly is," Sean said brightly. "I saw Mrs. Brody bringing Samantha. Is everything okay?"

"Fine. She's fine. None the worse for yesterday's trauma."

"Who? Samantha or Mrs. Brody?"

Rachel laughed. "Actually, both of them. Hannah'd been having some trouble with her health but she's better today. And Samantha is wearing a pretty new dress, so I'm sure she feels better, too."

"That's great. Well, guess I'd better get to work." Sean turned to go, then paused. "Oh, by the way, I stopped at Slocum's to gas up my car this morning and had a nice, informative talk with your friend, Craig. You'll be glad to hear he's not going to murder me, after all."

No, but I may. "What *kind* of nice talk?"

"Oh, nothing much. I just assured him I wasn't dating you. He seemed pretty relieved. The guy's still nuts about you. Maybe you should give him another chance."

Watching her expression harden, her lips press into a thin line, Sean was beginning to get the idea she was anything but pleased he'd made peace with Craig. He leaned to one side as if studying her pearl earrings.

"Oops."

"Oops, what?" Rachel absently fingered each stud and found nothing amiss.

"I think I see steam coming out of your ears."

"That's highly possible."

"Then, this must be my cue to exit. See ya!"

"Not if I see you first," Rachel muttered. To her surprise and chagrin, Sean grinned back at her.

"I should warn you. I have excellent hearing," he said.

Embarrassed, Rachel felt warmth infuse her cheeks. "Just as long as you can't read my thoughts."

"Would I like what I learned if I could?"

"That would depend upon whether you'd minded your own business lately," she told him. "As they say around here, 'If it ain't broke, don't fix it.'"

Sean continued to grin at her. "Ah, another bit of folk wisdom for my files. I'll make a special note of it. Thanks."

She would have loved to come up with a witty retort to put him in his place and give herself the last word. Unfortunately, no insightful gems popped into her head.

Slamming the classroom door she leaned her back against it and fought to steady her ragged breathing. What was it about that particular man that set her nerves on edge? He'd been nothing but pleasant to her—even helpful—yet half the time she found herself snapping at him as if they were sworn enemies. Life was too short, too precious, for that kind of attitude toward anyone. Besides, it wasn't her nature to be shrewish. If anything, she was too easygoing, too accepting of those who marched to a different drummer.

Some of that attitude she'd learned by becoming involved in a local church that welcomed everyone equally, no matter what their social or financial status. And some had come directly from her late father. In Rachel's opinion, any man who could put up with Martha Woodward for over thirty years was a candidate for sainthood.

"I still miss you, Daddy," she whispered, looking wistfully at the children milling around in the classroom. *And if I miss you, how much worse must it be for a child like Samantha? She lost both parents at once. No wonder she feels the need to imagine angels watching over her.*

Rachel blinked back unshed tears of empathy. More than once she'd wished for a similarly comforting vision. Like the day her stalwart father had passed away unexpectedly when she was hardly more than a child herself.

Or the night Craig had informed her he wasn't going to marry any woman who couldn't promise to give him the sons he needed to carry on his family name.

Chapter Six

Completing that first week of the fall semester left Rachel so drained she almost didn't get up early enough on Sunday to make it to church. If she hadn't laid out a favorite jacketed sundress the night before, she might not have managed to pull herself together in time.

Sunday school was nearly over when she dashed through the door to the main sanctuary and plopped down in a rear pew to wait for the morning worship service to begin. She'd barely caught her breath when her mother joined her, accompanied by Hannah Brody.

"Mom! Hi." Rachel gave Martha a brief hug, then glanced past her to speak to the other woman, too. "Good morning, Hannah. How are you?"

"Fair to middlin'," the heavy-set woman said.

"Did you bring Samantha with you?"

"Sure did. If there ever was a kid needed Sunday school teachin', it's that one. She's 'bout to drive me crazy."

Rachel leaned closer and took care to speak very softly. "Is she still seeing things?"

"That, and more," the foster mother said. "Now she's sayin' that you and that Bates fella are angels, too! I've never seen the like."

"Me? An angel?" Rachel snickered. "Not hardly."

Martha was smiling, too. "I can vouch for that."

"Thanks, Mom."

"Anytime. Want me to have a talk with the little girl and tell her what a trial it's been to raise you?"

"I think we can skip that much frankness," Rachel said with mock cynicism. "Teachers are supposed to set good examples. I wouldn't want you to destroy my positive image."

"Of course not." Martha reached over and patted her daughter's hand. "Hannah tells me that that poor baby has been through some heavy trials. I suppose it's natural for her to latch on to you. I'm glad you can be there for her."

Martha's sentence had trailed off, leaving Rachel wondering what had remained unspoken. She prodded, "But…?"

Sighing, Martha stared off at the distant altar as if making a decision, then answered. "But, you need to remember that you can't always be a part of her life the way you are now. It's not wise to let yourself get too attached to any of your students, honey. I've seen you do it before. Letting them go when the year is over is always a lot harder on you than it is on them.''

"If I didn't have compassion, I wouldn't be nearly as good at my job.''

"Maybe so. And maybe the opposite is true.'' Martha took her daughter's hand. "You also need to be fair. Can you really do that if you're overly fond of one or two of your students?''

"I'm not overly fond of anybody,'' Rachel argued. "My whole class is important to me. Teaching is my life. I wish I could make you understand that.''

"I do understand it,'' Martha replied. "I felt the same way when I was your age. My job at the county clerk's office gave me a wonderful sense of accomplishment—and more money than I'd ever had growing up. Looking back, I'm still thankful I worked there, but not for those same reasons.''

"I know. That's where you met Dad.'' Rachel had heard many versions of the story and they all led to the same conclusion.

"Yes. But that isn't what I'm trying to say this time. Things change. People change. Chances for added happiness come and go. If I hadn't met your father, I wouldn't have you.'' She smiled wistfully. "And I wouldn't give *that* up for anything. Until

you've had children of your own, you'll never understand how special you are to me.''

Children, again. Rachel's heart twisted. Buried dis-
appointment gave her voice a sharper edge than she'd
intended when she said, ''If you wanted grandchildren, Mom, you should have let me have the brothers
and sisters I kept asking for.'' The distressed look that
suddenly came over Martha was a surprise.

Glancing beyond her mother, Rachel saw Hannah
give a barely perceptible shake of unspoken warning.

Thoughtful, Rachel sat back in the pew, eyes forward and hands folded in her lap as if the service had
already begun. *How odd.* In all the times she and
Martha had argued the merits of motherhood, she'd
never seen her get teary-eyed before. Was it possible
she'd wanted more than one child?

Was it possible she'd been unable to conceive a
second time? Or a first? Rachel's breath caught. *Was
I adopted?*

Her head snapped around and she stared at Martha.
No, that wasn't the problem. It couldn't be. She and
her mother looked enough alike to be sisters, taking
into account their age difference. So why was her
mom suddenly acting upset? Too bad this wasn't the
right time or place to ask.

Resigned to wonder, at least for the present, Rachel
glanced at her watch, then smiled at the women beside her. ''It's getting late. I think I'll wander down
the hall toward the Sunday school rooms and pick up

Samantha so she doesn't get lost in the rush. Be back in a flash.''

Rather than give anyone a chance to object, she quickly got to her feet. The sanctuary was filling up, as usual, and there was a hum of muted conversation as families milled around in the aisles, searching for enough unoccupied space so they could all sit together.

Being short, Rachel couldn't see past the nearest parishioners. She smiled, offered an all-inclusive ''Excuse me,'' and stepped out into the crowded center aisle.

Someone jostled her. Touched her arm from behind. Her first thought was that Sean Bates had changed his mind and come to church, after all! Excited in spite of herself, she turned and looked up with an expectant, jubilant smile.

The smile quickly faded. Standing there, grinning down at her like a sated cat with bird feathers still clinging to its whiskers, was Craig Slocum.

Rachel was deeply grateful that her concern for Samantha had provided a ready-made excuse to gracefully escape from Craig. His smug expression had instantly made her so furious she doubted she'd have been able to come up with anything else socially acceptable.

By the time she reached the kindergarten Sunday school room she'd pulled herself together. Most of the children had already left. She peered in the open door. Samantha had stayed behind and was helping the teacher straighten the chairs.

"Hi," Rachel said, smiling.

Samantha's eyes widened. She squealed, "Miss Rachel!" forgot everything else and raced across the room.

Rachel bent down to welcome the child and was immediately caught in a possessive embrace. Samantha's thin arms wound around her neck and she clung as if she planned never to let go.

"I'm glad to see you, too," Rachel said. She straightened with the little girl in her arms and balanced the extra weight on one hip. "Did you like Sunday school?"

"Uh-huh. How come you're not my teacher?"

"I am. In regular school. Don't you want me to have a little time off?"

"I guess so." Samantha's eyes remained bright and curious. "Is this where you live?"

"At church?" Rachel laughed softly, her tone gentle. She was used to having students ask her if she lived at the school because that was where she was every time they saw her, but she'd never been asked if she lived at the church. "No, honey. I live in a regular house. Why?"

"Just wondered."

"Oh." Remembering Hannah's earlier mention of Samantha's angel fixation, Rachel assumed that might be the underlying reason for the question. Since angels were spiritual beings, they might live in a church—it was a logical conclusion for a five-year-old.

"Would you like Mrs. Brody to bring you to see my house someday? I have a dog, Schatzy, you could play with."

"You have a dog? Really?"

"Yes. And a cat. Muffin. But she's pretty old so she isn't nearly as much fun. She gets kind of grumpy sometimes."

"Mrs. Brody is old, too."

Amused, Rachel followed the childish reasoning. "And grumpy?"

"Sometimes."

"Well, I know she doesn't mean to be."

"I wish I could come live with you," Samantha said. Her grasp on Rachel's neck tightened.

"I'm afraid that's impossible. If I took my whole class home with me, poor Schatzy would go crazy. Besides, you see me in school every day."

"What if I have to move? I do that a lot, since…"

"I know, honey," Rachel said, gently stroking her back to comfort her. "Don't worry, okay? Everything will be fine."

"Promise?" There was a quaver in Samantha's voice.

"I promise."

Rachel knew she had no business promising happiness to anyone, let alone a child caught in the midst of life's trials. Yet she couldn't help herself. Not in this case. There was no way to make a five-year-old understand that sometimes bad things happened for good reasons. Convincing grown-ups of that concept was hard enough, even though it had a basis in scripture.

"Humph," Rachel mumbled as she made her way back to the pew where her mother and Hannah waited. *Grown-ups is right. I believe that God is in charge of my life, yet half the time I don't understand why bad things have to happen, so how can I hope to explain it to anyone else, let alone a child?*

She looked up. Her steps slowed. *Speaking of bad things…* Apparently, it wasn't even safe to come to church anymore. Not with her mother and Mrs. Brody in the same congregation.

Assessing the situation, Rachel stared. Martha and Hannah had scooted farther into the pew to make more room. The problem was, Craig was now sitting with them and the only empty space left was right next to him! Well, it was going to *stay* empty.

Continuing to hold Samantha, she approached the others. "I've decided to take my little friend to Children's Church."

"You're coming back, aren't you?" Martha asked with a sidelong glance toward Craig.

"Probably not," Rachel said. "You know me. I get along with kids better than I do with adults. I'll probably stay to help whoever is running the program this morning.''

That said, she spun around and headed back down the aisle toward the haven beyond the official sanctuary. There was nothing wrong with worshiping the Lord in the company of children, she assured herself. After all, their faith was pure, not all cluttered up with ritual and hidden agendas the way many adults' was.

"Mine included," she murmured.

Samantha noticed. "What?"

"Nothing, honey." Rachel gave her a parting hug, bent to set her back on her feet, then released her and took her hand. "Come on. You and I are going to a special church service just for kids."

"I know," the child told her, looking up with innocent adoration. "Angels always do."

By the time the main worship service concluded and Rachel rejoined her mother, Craig was nowhere to be seen. She couldn't help showing relief.

"Here's your purse and your Bible," Martha said, holding them out. "You left them here when you ran off."

"I didn't run anywhere," Rachel said. "I walked."

"There's more ways to run than with your feet," her mother argued. "Well, no matter. Craig's long gone. You missed your chance."

"Thank heavens for small favors."

Martha sighed. She eyed the petite blond girl clinging to her daughter's hand and gazing up at her lovingly. "Speaking of small, how did you two like Children's Church?"

"We had a lovely time, didn't we, Samantha?"

The child nodded.

"Hannah and I were talking about going out for Sunday dinner at Linden's Buffet," Martha said. "Would you like to join us?"

"What about Hank?" Rachel asked. She knew Hannah's husband well enough to be sure he wouldn't appreciate being left out of any meal, let alone an all-you-can-eat buffet.

"Went fishin' out to the lake," Hannah said. "Serves him right for leavin' me home alone. 'Sides, he took every bit o' the chicken I'd fried. Didn't even leave me a cold ole drumstick."

"In that case, I think you definitely deserve a restaurant meal," Rachel said, smiling. "I'd love to come along." She felt the child's grip on her hand tighten. "We both would. Wouldn't we, Samantha?"

"Okay," Hannah said. "But she rides with me. That's the rules. I been at this fostering business long enough to know better'n to break 'em." She held out a hand. "Come on, Sam. Let's go."

The little girl hesitated. Rachel looked down kindly. "She's right, honey. She's responsible for you. I'll meet you at the restaurant. I promise."

Instead of arguing as she'd expected, Samantha went straight to Hannah. *She trusts me,* Rachel thought. *Completely. And because of that she also trusts Hannah.* That was a new development, a very welcome one.

Rachel's eyes met the foster mother's, paused, then went to Martha's. Understanding flowed among them. Everyone knew what had just happened. Rachel rejoiced. What better place than in church to learn that her efforts were being rewarded.

And what better place to give thanks. She blinked slowly, reverently, silently grateful for the clear confirmation that she was doing the right thing in regard to the lonely child. No matter what anyone said, she knew she'd been meant to help Samantha. And that was exactly what she intended to continue doing.

Linden's Buffet was located in a strip mall in East Serenity, well away from the older part of town. On Sunday mornings the restaurant opened at eleven to accommodate the after-church crowd, then closed early. With such a brief window of opportunity, the buffet was always swamped, especially right after noon.

Martha rode over with Hannah and Samantha. Rachel thought it would be best to reinforce the foster mother's authority by driving separately. Slowed by the only traffic light in the entire town and unable to find a parking place on her first circuit through the Linden's lot, she entered a few minutes after the others. They'd already been seated. Samantha and Hannah were on one side of the table. Martha was alone on the other.

Breathless and grinning, Rachel joined them. "Whew! Thanks for saving me a seat. I've never seen this place so busy."

Martha made a face. "You don't get out much, do you."

"Not on Sunday mornings. You know very well I usually go straight home after church, change clothes and work in the yard. My garden gets away from me if I don't." Her smile widened. "Which reminds me. I have another batch of ripe zucchini for you, Mom."

"Oh, goody." There was no doubt of the older woman's sarcasm.

Rachel giggled. "I knew you'd be thrilled. I suppose I can spare a few vine-ripened tomatoes to go with it, providing you'll promise to take the squash off my hands, too."

"'Course I will." Martha winked at Hannah. "The last squashes she gave me were big enough to use as baseball bats!"

"I'll take some if you really have too many," Hannah said.

"Sure do." Rachel laughed at the scrunched-up face Samantha was making. She leaned closer to say, "It's very good for you," but the child's expression didn't improve. Obviously, there were some barriers that even a pseudo-angel couldn't overcome, zucchini consumption being one of them.

"Well, shall we go fill our plates before all the food is gone?" she asked.

"I'll wait here with the purses and order our drinks when the waitress finally gets around to us," Hannah offered. She gave the little girl beside her a pat and a kindly smile. "You can go ahead with Miss Rachel if you want to, Sam."

Rachel mouthed a silent *Thank you,* and held out her hand. Samantha immediately latched on to it, and they both followed Martha toward the steaming buffet tables.

"I'm going to start with salad," Rachel said, looking down at the child to check her reaction. It was predictably negative.

"Not me," Martha said, grinning. "I'm going straight for the pizza and the Mexican stuff, like tacos." She reached out toward the child. "Anybody who doesn't want to eat rabbit food can come with me."

Samantha didn't ask Rachel, she merely looked up at her to request permission with her eyes.

"Go ahead," Rachel told her. "I don't mind."

The child shyly accepted the older woman's hand. Watching them walk off together, Rachel was struck with an impression: her mother behaving like a grandmother. She would make a wonderful one, wouldn't she. No wonder she was so eager to see the next generation come into being.

"What I need to find is a man who already has

kids,'' Rachel muttered under her breath. ''Like that Mitch guy Brianne Bailey married last year.''

The biggest problem was the scarcity of handsome, eligible widowers with small children. It had been years since Rachel had encountered anyone who fit that description—and she was in the perfect job to spot such a man because she'd probably meet his children first.

Slowly filling her salad plate, she let her mind wander. It wasn't until Martha hurried over and grabbed her arm that she realized she'd been holding up the line by daydreaming.

''Did you see her?'' Martha asked.

''See who?''

''Samantha. One second she was right next to me and the next she was gone.''

Rachel frowned, forced herself to concentrate. ''Calm down, Mom. What do you mean, she's gone? She can't be gone. She wouldn't just leave us like that.''

''Then, she's been kidnapped! Oh dear. Oh my. It's all my fault. I only took my eyes off her long enough to pick up a slice of pizza.''

''She hasn't been kidnapped,'' Rachel assured the panicky woman. ''She's around here somewhere. She has to be. Maybe she went back to Hannah. Come on. Let's start by looking there.''

Though she was outwardly calm, Rachel couldn't

help the telltale tremor in her hands as she carried her salad to their table and set it at her place.

Hannah asked, "Where's Sam?"

"We were hoping you'd know," Rachel said. "She was with Mom a second ago, then she disappeared. I thought maybe she'd come back to you."

The portly woman stiffened and began to scan the surrounding tables. "Nope. I haven't seen her."

By this time, Martha was near tears. She sank into her chair with a moaned "Oh, no."

"All right," Rachel said, taking charge. "Mom, you and Hannah keep an eye on the front door. I'll go check the bathrooms. If she's not in there, I'll find the manager and get us some help."

Whirling, she managed to take one quick step before crashing into the man who had quietly approached behind her.

Rachel gasped. "Oh—" It was Sean! And Samantha was holding his hand.

"Now, now," he warned, smiling. "Watch your language. There are children present."

"I wasn't going to say anything bad. At least, not until I got a chance to talk to you alone," Rachel snapped. She gestured to include Hannah and Martha. "Do you have any idea how badly you scared us all?"

"Me? I just came in for a peaceful meal and got dragged over to your table." Still smiling, he looked down at his five-year-old companion. "It probably surprised me as much as it did you." He stepped up to the table and nodded an all-inclusive greeting. "Hello."

Rachel took over the introductions. "You remember Mrs. Brody," she said. "And this lady who looks like she's about to faint dead away is my mother, Martha Woodward. Mom, this is Sean Bates. We work together at the school."

Her mother proceeded to look Sean over, all the way from his sport shirt to the toes of his loafers. To Rachel's chagrin, Martha was acting as if she thought she'd seen the poor man's picture on a wanted poster and was trying to decide whether or not to turn him in and claim the reward money!

Finally, the older woman conceded. "Hello, Mr. Bates. I've heard about you. You're not from around here, are you?"

"No, ma'am. I'm from—"

Rachel purposely interrupted as he and Martha shook hands. "He's just moved to Serenity, Mom. Now that you two have met, if you don't mind, I'd like to eat. I'm starving."

"Oh dear. I was so dithered when Samantha ran off, I think I left my plate over there. I'd best go get it. I'll be right back."

"I'll go, too," Hannah said. She slowly pushed herself to her feet and ambled off, leaving Rachel and Samantha alone with Sean. The little girl continued to grasp his hand.

"And I'd better go see if I can find an empty table," Sean said, scanning the crowd. "This place came highly recommended, but nobody warned me I'd better get here early."

"Most churches let out at noon," Rachel explained. "You have to think like a Southerner to figure out our schedule. Which, by the way, is why I stopped you from telling Mom you're from Cleveland."

"I wondered why you'd interrupted me like that."

"Because you were about to admit to being a Yankee. Mom was already upset with you. I didn't see any reason to compound the problem."

"Are you serious?"

"Very. Arkansas may be considered the Midwest by some folks but it's the South to us. We're not all as set in our ways as my mother is, but it's still best to let people get to know you before you announce that you're from up north."

"That's unbelievable."

"I know. Humor the old-timers, okay? They're not mean. They're really sweet people. They're just proud of their heritage."

Samantha tugged on Sean's hand. When he looked down, she said, "You can sit by me."

"Well, I…"

What choice did Rachel have? Since she'd just gotten through extolling Southern manners and virtues, how could she gracefully counter the child's invitation and send him away?

"I suppose we can add another place," Rachel told him.

"I don't want to be a bother."

Too late for that. "There's an extra chair right over there. Bring the silverware, too, so we don't have to ask the waitresses for it. They have enough trouble keeping up with their customers on Sundays."

Sean checked with those seated at the neighboring table and got their permission to remove an empty chair. He was about to settle it in a place farther from Rachel, when Samantha took over and started tugging. The chair's legs collided with those of others—and of people—as she struggled to work it between the closely placed tables.

"Say 'Excuse me' when you bump into somebody," Sean told the eager little girl.

"'Scuse me," she announced loudly, speaking to no one in particular while continuing to awkwardly tug on the chair.

"Here. Let me do that," Sean said. "Where are we going with this?"

Samantha was beaming. She pointed. "Over there. By me."

Since the child's place was directly across from Rachel's, that left only the space at the end of the table for Sean, which meant he'd be seated between them with little elbow room. Judging by the look on the teacher's face, she wasn't pleased.

"Tell you what, Samantha," he said lightly. "Let's put you here, on the end, because you won't take up as much space as I do, and I'll sit in your chair. That way you can be right next to Miss Rachel, too."

"Okay!" Samantha hopped into the chair Sean had been carrying as soon as he slid it into place.

His glance caught Rachel's and held it. "Is that better?"

"Fine. Whatever. It makes no difference to me." Giving a shrug she glanced at her untouched salad. "Since I seem to be the only one who's managed to find anything to eat yet, why don't you two go fill your plates. I'll hold the fort till everybody gets back."

"Sounds good to me," Sean said. He held out a hand. Samantha grabbed it and jumped down.

"Watch her every second," Rachel warned as they started away. "When Mom tried to take her to the buffet table, she ran off and picked up a stray. No telling who or what she might bring back next time."

The noise level in the room kept Rachel from hearing Sean's reply with his back turned, but the slight, rhythmic shaking of his shoulders told her he was laughing.

Chapter Seven

It didn't take Rachel long to decide she'd have been just as well off to allow Sean to sit next to her as to have him directly in her line of sight. She couldn't continue to stare at her plate and ignore the pleasant dinner conversation around her forever. Soon, somebody was bound to question her inordinate interest in her food. Every time she raised her gaze, however, there was Sean, seeming larger than life and definitely paying way too much attention to her.

I'm being ridiculous, Rachel told herself. *I'm not afraid of him. Or of my mother's interference.* The two elements brought together, however, might prove embarrassing, especially if Martha ever got it into her head that Sean Bates would be a good candidate to take Craig's place. Or, worse, that both men might make suitable sons-in-law!

Rachel was about to excuse herself early, on the pretext of needing to get home, when Samantha announced, "I'm gonna go see Miss Rachel's dog. It got shot."

Martha was so astounded she grabbed her daughter's forearm and almost caused her to drop her fork. "What? You never told me about that!"

"There's nothing to tell," Rachel insisted with a puzzled frown. "I don't know where she got such an idea. I just said she could come and visit. I never said Schatzy was hurt."

Sean began to chuckle. "Listen to yourself. I know exactly why Samantha is confused."

"Of course!" Rachel rolled her eyes. "I said Schatzy and she heard something else." Leaning closer to the wide-eyed child, she explained, "Schatzy is his name, honey. He hasn't been shot. He's fine."

"Really?"

"Really."

"Are you still gonna make me cupcakes?"

Though Rachel had always prided herself on figuring out the convoluted reasoning of young children, she was lost again. "Cupcakes? I don't remember saying anything about that, either."

"Uh-huh. You did so," the little girl insisted.

"Okay. If you're sure."

To her right, Martha was giggling behind her napkin. "I'll bet she means your cat this time."

Sighing and nodding, Rachel had to admit her mother was probably right. "Are you thinking of *muffins,* honey?"

"Yeah. Those. With frosting."

The image that that suggestion brought to Rachel's mind made her laugh, too. "I wasn't talking about baking anything, Samantha. My cat's name is Muffin. I'm afraid she wouldn't like it much if we spread frosting all over her."

"Oh." The five-year-old's lower lip was starting to quiver and moisture was pooling in her bright blue eyes.

"But you can help me feed her if you want," Rachel offered quickly. "Muffin loves to eat. And Schatzy loves to play ball. Maybe Mrs. Brody will let you come over this afternoon. Once you get to know my animals, you won't get their names mixed up again."

A tear trickled down Samantha's cheek as she looked at her foster mother and asked in a quavering voice, "Can I?"

That emotional plea would have melted a heart of stone—and Hannah Brody's was as soft as a marshmallow to start with. "Don't see why not. Hank's not due home yet, and I've got no chores to do till he drags in a mess o' fish—if he catches any." She looked across at Rachel. "Okay if we stop by your place on the way home from here and save me a trip back? I have to drop your mama off, anyway, so we'll be right close.''

"Sure," Rachel said. "It's pretty hot to be running around outside in the yard, but Samantha and Schatzy can play fetch in my hallway without hurting anything."

Samantha brightened. "Goody! *Everybody* can go."

Before she could stop herself, Rachel's gaze snapped up and locked with Sean's. *Everybody?* Oh, that certainly wasn't what she'd had in mind when she suggested they stop by her house on their way home from dinner.

Smiling, Sean said, "You have that deer-in-the-headlights look, Rachel. Don't worry. I'm not inviting myself. I have plenty of things of my own to do today."

"Like what?" Martha asked sweetly.

"Well, I..."

"Just as I thought," she said, clearly pleased with herself. "You haven't lived in Serenity long enough to be involved in much besides your work at the school. If you get bored at my daughter's you can always come over to my house for a glass of sweet tea or lemonade. I only live a couple of blocks from her."

"Thank you, ma'am, but I really can't."

"Nonsense. You and I can have a nice chat. I've been wanting to ask you more about your background, anyway. Are your people related to the Bates family that founded Batesville?''

''I doubt that very much, ma'am.'' His glance at Rachel was an unspoken appeal for rescue.

Rachel knew exactly how he felt. There was only one thing to do—provide a distraction. She jumped to her feet and abruptly changed the subject. ''Today's dessert is pineapple cake. I'm going to go get mine. I'll bring some for everybody. Come on, Sean. You can help me carry the extra plates.''

Without waiting for a reply, she started off, weaving between the tables like a skier headed down a slalom course. It wasn't necessary to turn around to know that Sean was right behind her. She could sense his presence in every nerve. Even the roots of her hair tingled.

He didn't speak until they reached the dessert table. ''Thanks.''

''For what?''

''For getting me away from your mother.''

Rachel chuckled softly. ''You're not away from her yet. Mom can be very persistent.''

''So I've gathered. Between her and Samantha, it looks like you and I will have our hands full.''

She handed him two small plates and balanced three others herself. ''No pun intended, but we already do—and I'm not talking about this cake.''

''How do you mean?''

''Life in a small town. I tried to warn you about it

before. You'll manage okay if you remember that only part of whatever you hear is true. Think of the rest as misunderstanding, embellishment, wishful thinking or downright lies. Mom usually falls into the 'wishful thinking' category.''

"What does that have to do with me?"

"Plenty. For instance, if you were foolish enough to stop by my place this afternoon when the others do, you'd just provide more grist for the rumor mill.''

"I see. And that would come between you and Craig?"

If Rachel hadn't been holding the dessert plates she'd have thrown her hands into the air in frustration. She did whirl to face Sean. "No! I already told you. There's *nothing* between me and Craig. It was over long ago.''

"Then, why did he try to sit by you in church this morning?"

"What…? How…?"

"Your mother told me. She can be very informative.''

"Terrific. Did she bother to mention that I didn't stay with them after he got there?"

"No. She left that part out. What happened?"

"I refused to be manipulated.''

"I see.''

Rachel arched an eyebrow as she studied his face. "Somehow, I doubt you do.''

"Oh, I don't know. It does prove that my first impression of him was right. The man's still interested in you. Otherwise, why did he act jealous when he saw us together? And why would he purposely face rejection by trying to sit with you and your mother this morning?''

"You're beginning to sound just like her."

"Sociable?"

"No, crazy."

Sean laughed. "You're not the first person who's told me that. And I doubt you'll be the last."

Rachel had never dreamed Sean would ignore her well-meant warning and show up at her house, anyway. True, Samantha's insistence that he come along had undoubtedly played a big part in his decision. What he wasn't considering, however, was what Rachel might have to endure as a result of his stubbornness.

To make matters worse, Hannah had opted to drop Samantha off to play with the dog first, then make a quick trip to take Martha home before returning to pick up the little girl.

"Okay. Outside," Rachel ordered when she realized she and Sean were about to be left alone with no one but the child for a chaperone. "Everybody on the front porch. Now."

Samantha's whining protests were not enough to change her mind. Only Muffin ignored the marching orders.

Acting pleased and relaxed, Sean sauntered outside and made himself at home on the glider, while Rachel plunked herself down on the top porch step with the little dachshund and Samantha. When the dog finally stopped trying to lick her face and rolled over in blissful submission, the child started scratching Schatzy's tummy.

"Is it always this hot this time of year?" Sean asked.

"No. Lots of times it's hotter." Rachel eyed the black sedan parked noticeably in her driveway. "It's your fault we have to sit out here."

"So the neighbors won't get the wrong impression, you mean?"

"Exactly."

Sean chuckled softly to himself. "Listening to you talk about Serenity makes me feel like I've been zapped back to the 1950s. I can't believe anyplace is actually as antiquated as you say this one is. Not these days."

"We aren't backward here, if that's what you mean. Maybe I am being too sensitive about gossip, but remember, I do teach impressionable children. I'm also a product of my mother's upbringing, so I'm bound to be at least half a bubble out of plumb."

"Half a what?"

"You know. Like, two sandwiches short of a picnic? Three bricks short of a load? A few squares shy of a whole quilt?"

When he continued to look confused, she explained further, gesturing for emphasis. "Picture a carpenter's level. The bubble inside the glass capsule has to be right in the middle, between the marks, to ensure that whatever he's building isn't crooked or leaning. Half a bubble out of plumb means 'not quite normal.'"

Sean grinned. "*That* I can understand."

"I thought you would."

"Of course, if you'd listened to my professors you wouldn't think any of us were normal. That's a pretty subjective term." He grew pensive. "If you were to ask my family, they'd swear they were the normal ones and I was the oddball."

"I take it you disagree."

"Yeah."

A scowl knit his brow, and Rachel could see the muscles of his jaw clenching. Apparently, their innocent conversation had touched a tender spot. "Want to tell me about it, Doc?"

"Mutual psychoanalysis?" Sean began to lose his angry look. "I don't think so."

"Why not? You might feel better if you unloaded."

"What makes you think I have anything to unload?"

"Your expression. Your attitude." Rachel smiled sweetly. "The way your mood changes the minute you mention your family."

"It's that obvious?"

"Sticks out like a sore thumb. How long have you been estranged from them?"

"I wouldn't put it that strongly. We just don't see eye to eye. I figured it would be best for everybody if I got away from them, at least for a while."

"Your parents?"

"And my brothers," he said with a slow nod.

"They're still in Cleveland?"

Another nod. "Dad runs a hardware store in the Heights. My brothers work for him."

"Maybe they're jealous that you went on to college?" Rachel suggested.

"No. We all had the same opportunities. Paul and Ian are both older than I am. They had degrees in business administration long before I got mine."

"Was that when you drove a school bus?"

Sean took a deep breath and released it slowly. "No. I didn't do that till I went back to school again later, after I was on my own."

"Which explains why you seem older than most recent college graduates."

He managed a wry smile. "Sometimes I feel downright ancient."

"Well, my offer stands. If you ever decide you need a real person to talk to, remember I'm available."

"Thanks but no thanks. I'm fine. I don't need anybody."

"Everybody needs somebody," Rachel countered.

"A friend, a mate, God. For me, it was the good Lord."

"Spoken like a true resident of the Bible Belt."

"That's absolutely right," she said, refusing to allow herself to become upset over his cynical tone. "And proud of it. There have been times in my life when I might have done something really stupid if I hadn't had my faith to fall back on."

"I don't need a crutch."

Rachel laughed lightly. "I'm not talking about stumbling along with a broken leg, Sean. I'm talking about being so uplifted, so enthralled with the wonders of life, you feel like your feet aren't even touching the ground."

Before he could answer, Samantha looked up from where she'd been playing, smiled at them both and said, "I know. Angels always fly like that."

If Schatzy hadn't jumped up and yipped, tail wagging, no one would have noticed Hannah's return a few minutes later.

She leaned out of the van and yelled at Samantha. "Come on, Sam. Hank's home. He caught me at Martha's. We gotta go."

"Awww…" The child immediately began to pout.

"You can come back another time," Rachel said firmly. "And we'll see each other in school tomorrow."

Acting as if there was no chance of her being disobeyed, she ushered the unhappy little girl to the van and helped her climb into a rear seat where she could be belted in for safety.

Rachel was standing in the driveway, waving good-bye and watching Hannah and Samantha drive away, before she fully realized she had one remaining guest. The uninvited one.

Her conscience added, *the lonely one.*

Oh, why had Sean revealed so much about his family?

Because you asked him, dummy, her heart answered. *You're a terrible softie who doesn't know enough to keep her mouth shut.*

That much was true. It was also true, however, that at least a portion of her empathy was a gift from God—a sensitivity that she knew He expected her to use to His glory.

Which didn't mean she was supposed to climb on her soapbox and start to preach, she reminded herself as she started back toward the porch where Sean waited. *Too bad.* It would have been a lot easier for her to lecture him, then walk away, than to continue to befriend him. Friendship meant personal involvement. Commitment. It also meant she'd probably have to reveal a portion of her inner self that few people ever saw, in order to show Sean it was safe to do the same.

"Why?" she muttered, casting her eyes heavenward. "Why me?"

Sean was already on his feet, waiting, as she approached the porch. "Sorry. I didn't catch that. What did you say?"

"Oh, nothing important. I was just talking to myself."

He chuckled. "Do you do that often?"

"All the time."

"I suppose you answer yourself, too."

"Uh-huh. Doesn't everybody?"

"No, but I promise not to tell the school board that you do it."

"Thanks." Rachel made a silly face at him and sighed. "Well, here we are. What now?"

To her surprise, his cheeks reddened as if he were blushing. Was that possible? She faced him boldly, fists on her hips, her head tipped to one side.

"A penny for your thoughts?"

"No way." His color deepened.

"That bad, huh?"

"You'd probably think so."

"Maybe not. You never know," she said.

Sean's resulting smile reminded her of the one Craig had displayed in church. That was *not* a good sign.

Rachel had remained at the top of the porch stairs. Sean approached her slowly, then passed by and took one step down. When he turned to face her, they were close to the same height.

"I was thinking about how beautiful you are," he said. "And I'm not talking about your looks."

"Hey, thanks a bunch."

He gently clasped her arms, holding her so she couldn't turn away. "I'm trying to give you a compliment, Rachel. You have the sweetest nature of anyone I've ever known."

Awed, she was speechless. Her eyes searched his for any sign of insincerity. There was none. Sean Bates might like to kid around a lot of the time, but right now he was being serious. Too serious.

Rachel managed a smile. At least, she thought she did. Given the charged atmosphere between her and Sean she wasn't positive of anything, least of all her own reactions. The sensation of his warm hands caressing her upper arms reminded her of the first time they'd accidentally touched—when he'd tried to open the office door for her. That unexpected encounter had nearly destroyed her composure, just when she'd needed her wits about her for Samantha's sake.

This time, however, there was no one to consider but herself. And Sean, of course. The intensity of his gaze made her toes curl, her pulse hammer. It took her breath away. Without giving the action any conscious thought she parted her lips. They were trembling slightly.

Sean saw the telling reaction and his heart overruled his head. He bent slowly, purposefully, giving Rachel time to order him to stop. She didn't. On the contrary, she closed her eyes, raised her chin and leaned closer.

Before he could change his mind and behave sensibly, he followed through and kissed her.

Chapter Eight

Rachel's eyes popped open the moment he ended the kiss. She stared up at him, dumbfounded.

If Sean hadn't kept holding on to her arms, she knew she would have crumpled into a little pile of nothingness at his feet the instant their lips met. Wouldn't *that* have impressed the neighbors! From intelligent schoolteacher to inert dust bunny in three seconds flat. Imagining that vivid illustration made her giggle.

Clearly puzzled, Sean studied her expression. "I've had my face slapped before, but this is the first time a woman has laughed at me for making a pass at her. Was I that funny?"

"No!" She tried to compose herself and failed. The giggles continued. "I— I think I'm just stressed. You know, with school starting, and my mother making waves, and Samantha's awful situation, and Craig showing up in church this morning, and, and…''

''I get it,'' Sean said. There was a tinge of wounded pride in his voice. ''One little kiss pushed you over the edge and now you're going to blame me if you end up getting hysterical.''

''Something like that.'' Rachel's grin was so broad her jaw ached. The hurt look on his face helped her decide to reach out and gently pat his cheek. ''Hey, don't sulk. It was a very, um, nice kiss. Really.''

'' 'Nice?' Is that all you can say?''

''Well…'' Once again, Sean's perturbed expression tickled her funny bone. ''Oh, all right. I liked it, okay? It was great. Stupendous. So wonderful I'm about to keel over in ecstasy.'' Which wasn't all *that* far from the truth.

He frowned as he released her. ''You don't have to exaggerate. I get the general idea.''

I'm grateful you don't, Rachel thought. She said, ''Well, good. I'm glad we have that all settled. Now, as I was saying before you got carried away—what next? Can I fix you a glass of iced tea or something?''

Sean took another step backward down the porch stairs, his hand sliding down the railing. ''No thanks. I think it's high time I left.''

It's long past *the time you should have left.* Instead of voicing that opinion she offered a plausible pretext. ''I do have quite a few chores to do before nightfall. Stopping at Linden's after church kind of messed up my schedule. I usually catch up on yard work Sunday afternoons.''

''I meant to tell you what a beautiful place you have,'' he said.

One more step took him to the level of the lawn, where he paused to casually scan her yard. There were low, lush flower beds lining the front of the house. Two shade trees between there and the street were ringed with bright pink and white blooms that stood out boldly against the strong green of the grass. If there were weeds hidden among the plantings, he certainly couldn't tell. The only chore he could see that looked like it needed doing was to mow the lawn.

''I suppose it does take quite a bit of work to keep everything looking just right,'' he said.

''Thank you. Yes. It does. But I enjoy puttering. Flowers never sass me like some kids do, or argue with me the way Mom does.'' *Or kiss me when I'm not expecting it.*

Sean struck a nonchalant pose, hands stuffed into the pockets of his slacks. ''So, what's on today's agenda?''

''I have to mow the—'' Rachel stopped herself the moment she saw an eager glint in his eyes. It was too late.

''That's what I figured. I'm a whiz at pushing a mower. Since it's partly my fault that you're late getting started, let me cut the grass for you.''

"I don't push my mower," she countered. "I ride around on it. Actually, it's lots of fun."

"Great!"

"I mean, it's fun for *me*. I like mowing the lawn."

"Honest?"

Rachel raised her right hand, palm out, as if taking a sworn oath. "Honest."

"Okay." Sean shrugged and started to turn away. "I'll see you tomorrow, then."

"Right. Tomorrow."

Watching him saunter to his car she was struck by how strongly she wanted him to stay. It wouldn't do to reveal that urge, of course. Now that she'd finally gotten him to agree to leave, she'd be twice the fool to ask him to change his mind and hang around longer. Still, the idea was appealing. Foolish, but appealing.

Sean wasn't sure why Rachel seemed so determined to get rid of him but he could tell when he wasn't wanted. Clearly, he'd overstayed his welcome—and then some.

He was getting into his car when a mud-splattered, red pickup truck came roaring down the middle of Old Sturkie Road and skidded to a stop at the end of the driveway, blocking his only exit. He tensed. Unless Rachel had other former jealous boyfriends he didn't know about, there was little doubt who had just arrived.

Staying focused on the truck for only a few seconds, Sean glanced back at the porch. Rachel was no longer smiling. She was standing her ground, yet clearly not thrilled to see Craig Slocum. One hand was clamped tightly to the stairway railing and the other was squeezed into a fist at her side.

Sean hesitated. There was no way he was going to drive off and leave Rachel at the mercy of the angry-looking man who was now climbing out of the red pickup and heading his way. Besides, as long as his car was penned in, he couldn't make a graceful exit even if he wanted to.

Slamming the car door, Sean welcomed his rival with a smile and an amiable ''Hello, again,'' his right hand extended.

Slocum didn't respond verbally. He merely closed the distance between them, gritted his teeth and swung.

The unexpected punch caught Sean off guard. He grabbed his chin and staggered back against the side of his car. Before he could gather himself for the me-lee he was sure was coming, Craig had spun around and stalked back to his pickup. The truck's tires squealed, throwing loose gravel, then caught.

Rachel ran up and grabbed Sean's arm as Craig sped away. ''Are you okay?''

''I think so.'' He gingerly wiggled his jaw. Surprisingly, it still worked.

''I can't believe he did that!''

''I can. I kept trying to tell you he was jealous.''

"I know, but... Why hit you? That's not fair. We've never given him any reason to..." She took a ragged breath. "Somebody must have seen you kiss me!"

"News travels *that* fast? I doubt it. Not even around here." Sean glanced up and down the narrow road. "I have an idea he was watching us himself."

"That's ridiculous." Shaking her head she studied Sean's face. "Move your hand and let me see your chin."

"I'm not sure I should let go of it until I decide if I'm still in one piece," he quipped, wincing. "Your boyfriend packs quite a wallop."

"I told you..."

"I know, I know. He's not your boyfriend. He means nothing to you. Maybe you should tell *him* instead of me. I don't think ole Craig has figured it out on his own."

"He should have. We had a big enough argument the night we broke up."

"Then, it's probably an ego thing. Most men are like that. We aren't exactly rational where our women are concerned." His eyes met Rachel's and darkened. "Figuratively speaking, of course."

"Of course." She looped her arm through his. "Come on. You and I are going into the house to put some ice on your face. Otherwise, you're liable to look like you were in a fight."

"I was," Sean gibed. "I just didn't find out about it in time to participate."

Looking up at him with a smile she said, "Oh, I think you participated plenty."

Seated at Rachel's kitchen table, Sean held a cold pack to his jaw as he watched her preparing fresh lemonade. She'd kicked off her shoes and was standing with her back to him, giving him the opportunity to enjoy looking at her without embarrassment.

He'd always thought of petite women as delicate, which she was, in a way. Yet she was also strong. Any lack of size was more than made up for by her spunky attitude and obvious intelligence.

When he started to grin, the pain in his cheek muted his good humor. If he was going to convince Rachel he was fine, it was apparently going to have to be done straight-faced.

"I could squeeze those lemons for you," Sean said. "The guy didn't cripple me, you know."

Rachel turned, pitcher in hand. "I know. But there's no need. I'm all done. If we finish this batch, you can squeeze the lemons for the next one, okay?"

"Sure." Sean tried a lopsided smile and was happy to find it didn't cause undue pain.

"What's so funny?"

"You are. The way you say things sometimes. I know you don't mean to, but it comes out sounding like you're talking to little kids."

"It doesn't!"

"Oh yes, it does. There's a kind of cajoling tone you use that reminds me of the way you deal with Samantha when she's pitching a fit."

"Oh dear."

Rachel placed the pitcher on the table, went to the cupboard to get tall glasses, then filled them with ice from the freezer before returning. She stood till she'd poured them each a glassful of lemonade, then sat down across from him.

"I think it's kind of cute," Sean told her.

"And I think I've been spending too much time exclusively with children."

"Possibly. You've definitely found your niche, though. I admire that. You know what you want to do and you do it. There are times when that can take a lot of courage."

"No kidding." She smiled over at him. "Speaking of courage, how's your face?"

Sean chuckled. "I hardly notice it." In order to drink he'd had to lay aside the towel they'd wrapped around the ice cubes to pad them. Now, he canted his chin toward her. "How does it look?"

"Kind of red. Could be from the cold instead of a bruise. We'll have to wait and see."

"Suppose it's too late for me to grow a beard to cover it?"

"Probably. Although I did notice a little stubble when—" She broke off, suddenly all too aware of the intimate way she'd caressed his cheek when she'd been so worried about his welfare.

"Yeah." He rubbed his hand over the unhurt side of his face. "I guess I do need a shave. Too bad my hair isn't darker, like my brother Paul's. He can go from clean-shaven to looking like a bum in a day."

Rachel had noticed a definite stiffening of her companion's posture as soon as he mentioned his brother. That was the second time. Whatever had distanced Sean from his family clearly had left hard feelings that he had yet to deal with.

"I like the color of your hair," Rachel said. "It's kind of brown and kind of red at the same time. Very unusual."

"My genealogy is part Irish and part German with some unknown ancestors thrown in for interest. Guess you could say I'm a mutt."

"We all are." She took a slow sip of her lemonade and licked her lips before continuing. "According to family legend, one of my great-great-great-grandmothers escaped from the Trail of Tears."

"When the Cherokees were marched across to Oklahoma?"

"That's the time. There were actually several different trails. The one that came through northern Arkansas was called Benge's Route, named after the army officer who was in charge of that detachment."

"How interesting."

"I thought so. There were supposedly about twelve-hundred Cherokees in that particular group, although nobody kept very accurate records of the tribes back then.''

''So, what makes you think your grandmother escaped?''

''Family legend. In those days, folks didn't talk openly about things like that, so there's really no way I can prove it—but I'd like to believe the story is true.''

''Can't you trace the genealogy somehow?''

''Not without more details. I don't even know her original name. I'm assuming she anglicized it. Supposedly, she hid out on a local farm till the army gave up looking for her. Later, she married a boy from around here and they lived way back in the hills where nobody bothered them.''

''That's fascinating.''

''I always thought so. And she wasn't the only one to break away from the band. Folks around here say that's why there are so many dark-haired, blue-eyed natives. There were a lot of blue-eyed Cherokee.''

''Really?'' Studying her face he noted—not for the first time—the striking effect of dark lashes shadowing the vivid blue of her eyes. ''I had wondered why your eyes aren't brown like your hair.''

He'd paid that much attention? Oh!

Rather than admit to herself that she was flattered, she continued with their discussion of history. ''I just wish the Native Americans hadn't been forced to hide their origins in order to live away from the reservation. Think of the stories they could have told.''

"They probably did pass on their oral history to some extent. Otherwise, you wouldn't have known anything about your ancestor.''

"That's true. So, tell me more about your family.''

"There's nothing to tell.''

"No skeletons in the closet? No big secrets?''

Sean huffed, gave her a derisive look. "The skeletons in my family are more likely to be found in a bar than in a closet.''

To Rachel's dismay he abruptly got to his feet and carried his half-empty glass to the sink.

"I'd better be going.''

"You should keep ice on that bruise,'' she cautioned.

"I have ice at home.''

"I know. But you still have to get from here to there. Where do you live, anyway?''

"East Serenity, in the new apartments. That's why I was eating at Linden's when we ran into each other. It's close to home.''

"I see.'' Rachel rolled the kitchen towel more tightly around what was left of the ice cubes she'd given him and held it out. "Here. Take this with you.''

"I don't need it.''

"Humor me.'' She was following him to the back door, towel in hand.

"Since when do you need humoring? I don't think I've ever seen you mad at anybody."

"I was plenty mad at Craig Slocum about half an hour ago."

Sean managed another crooked smile. "I wasn't too crazy about him, either. Next time, remind me to duck."

"If I have to remind you," Rachel said with a soft laugh, "maybe he hit you harder than we thought."

"It wasn't bad. I've taken lots worse."

The comment hadn't been specific, yet she couldn't help assuming he was still referring to his family. Though she hadn't grown up with siblings, she had had friends with brothers and sisters. They'd never admitted that rivalry within the family had led to physical clashes, but she knew that kind of thing happened. It was certainly more likely among boys.

And, as the youngest, Sean might have been cast as the scapegoat. That unfortunate tendency was one she'd dealt with before in her students. It wasn't all that rare for one child to be singled out to bear the brunt of an angry parent's outbursts, which often led siblings to behave in a similar fashion and produced an atmosphere of ongoing abuse.

Rachel laid her hand on his arm to stop him as he started through the open door. When he looked down at her, whatever she'd intended to say fled from her mind and was replaced by "There's only one place to find unconditional love and acceptance, Sean."

She hadn't meant for her concern to be so evident or for her words to be so bold. In truth, she'd had no forewarning that she was going to say anything that alluded to God's perfect love. Which was just as well. If she had planned to present a plea for her Christian faith she'd probably have gotten so uptight she'd have stammered something unintelligible and ruined the whole thing.

His frown wasn't as puzzled as it was off-putting.

"If you mean *church,* you can forget it. I already told you that."

"No, not church." Smiling benevolently, Rachel shook her head. "You don't have to be in a special building to open yourself to the possibilities God offers. Jesus said that all the time. I know it seems far-fetched to think that a Heavenly Father can love you just the way you are, but I happen to know from experience that He can and does."

"Right. I suppose you believe in Santa Claus and the Tooth Fairy, too."

"I used to. Then I grew up and searched for the truth myself. Faith isn't a gift I can just hand you, or I would. It's an inside job. Like love. You can't see that, either, but you believe it exists, don't you?"

"Maybe. Maybe not." He pushed through the door. Before turning to head for his car he said, "Thanks for the lemonade. I know you were risking your reputation by taking me in to doctor me. I appreciate it."

"No problem. The next time you get clobbered you'll know where to come for first aid." To her relief, that quip brought his crooked smile back.

"I don't intend to stand still and be Craig's punching bag again," Sean said firmly. "There aren't any more unhappy guys waiting to deck me, are there? I hate surprises like that."

"Nope. He's it. One's enough, don't you think?"

"One is plenty." Sean backed away toward his waiting car.

Schatzy followed, barking bravely and nipping at the air by Sean's ankles, as if his ridiculous efforts were the real reason the man was leaving.

When Rachel caught up to the little dachshund she scooped him into her arms for safekeeping and held him close while he wiggled, stretched and licked at her earlobe in pure adoration.

"I'm glad he's not a mastiff," Sean said as he started the car.

"Me, too. He'd be awfully hard to cuddle if he was."

"Right."

Watching Sean back out of the driveway, she wondered if the redness on his cheeks was from the blow he'd received or if he was blushing again, simply because she'd mentioned cuddling.

Either way, she was the cause, Rachel reasoned.

To her chagrin, that concept didn't bother her nearly as much as she thought it should.

Chapter Nine

By the following morning, Sean's face showed little sign that he'd been punched. He did notice a few school staff members whispering and sneaking peeks at him, but he figured that was normal, given his newcomer status. Moving to any strange area would have been the same. Serenity might be a tight-knit community, but there wasn't anyplace that didn't have its cliques. Here, they just didn't make any bones about it.

Sean chuckled to himself. He'd only been in town for a week or so, yet he'd long ago lost count of the number of times someone had looked him up and down and drawled, "You aren't from around here, are you?" It was as if he'd had "Outsider" tattooed across his forehead!

Well, at least he finally had an office—of sorts.

Vanbruger had had maintenance clear out a large storage closet directly behind the main offices and had fit it with a desk, chair and single upright filing cabinet. It was certainly not much, but he couldn't fault the school district for that. He'd known when he applied for the counselor's job that it was a part-time position, which was why he'd suggested he become their standby bus driver. Chances were good he'd been hired partly because of his versatility.

He'd removed his jacket and was trying to decide how best to arrange the cramped room, when a knock on the door startled him. "Yes?"

Rachel opened the door, stuck her head through, looked around and grinned. "Hey, cozy."

"You could call it that." He dusted off his hands. "Come on in. I'll give you the fifty-cent tour."

She obliged, laughing softly. "I don't think it should cost more than a dime at the most." Crossing to his desk in three steps, she ran her hand over the scarred surface. "Nice furniture. I love antiques. Where did they get this one?"

"From storage, I assume," Sean said. "I've already cleaned a mouse nest out of the bottom drawer." The memory of all the dust made his nose itch again and he sneezed.

Rachel had circled the desk and was pretending to admire it. "How lovely. It came with its own science project. Just like my refrigerator."

"You have mice in your refrigerator?"

"No, silly. Science projects. You know, moldy things I can't identify that have gotten shoved to the back of a shelf and been overlooked."

"Whew." Sean made a face and pretended to wipe his brow. "I'm glad you explained. I ate something you fixed from that refrigerator and I was getting worried."

"You didn't eat, you drank," Rachel said.

"Lemonade," he added. "I drank lemonade. When you just say I *drank,* it sounds like you mean something else."

"Sorry." She studied him out of the corner of her eye while she made a point of looking elsewhere. "You have a nice view from here, too."

To her delight, that ridiculous observation made Sean laugh. "I think you have to work here longer than I have to rate a window. I thought I might get one of those fake ones. You know, the frame is real and then you put an outdoor scene behind it so it looks like you do have a view."

"Well, don't buy one," Rachel said quickly. "When I remodeled my house I stacked all the old wooden window sashes out behind the toolshed. You can come pick out whatever you want from the pile and we can rig it to hang." She rapped on the paneling. "This sounds hollow. Maybe you should screw the frame right to the wall for support."

"Uh-huh." He sighed pensively. "Too bad I don't have access to power tools the way I used to at the store. It would be much easier to drill holes for the screws.''

"I have lots of tools at home. You're welcome to borrow anything you need.''

"You do?''

She found his amazement amusing. "Yes, I do. Why? Did you think men were the only ones allowed to own tools?''

"Not exactly. It's just hard for me to picture you with a framer's hammer in your hand, banging in sixteen-penny nails.'' Pausing, he added, "Sixteen-penny is a size, not the cost per nail.''

"I know that.'' Rachel made a face at him. "You have a lot to learn about country girls, mister. Some of us even drive tractors and help with the haying before we're out of grade school.''

"Did you do that?''

"Well, no. But I have friends who did. The closest my folks got to farming was to keep some beef cows and raise a few calves every year. We either traded for what little hay we needed or bought it. Most of the time there's plenty of grass for grazing, as long as you don't run too many head on a small plot of land.''

Sean offered her his only chair. When she chose to remain standing, he perched on the edge of the battered desk. "I can see I have a lot to learn. The kids won't respect my advice in other areas if I come across as ignorant about things like farming.''

"Don't worry. You're bright. You'll catch on," Rachel assured him. "And you'll be able to give them pointers about someday surviving in a big city."

"I suppose a lot of them do leave here once they're grown."

"Not as many as you'd think. Some go away to college, of course. I've found that the majority of the families who've lived in the Ozarks for generations try to talk their kids into staying fairly close by. Kind of like your father did when he involved you and your brothers in his business. What made you pull away, anyway?"

Sean got to his feet and circled the desk. When he was on the opposite side he turned and faced her. His jaw was set, his gaze penetrating. "You might as well stop bringing up my family, Rachel. I never should have mentioned the store or my brothers in the first place. I don't intend to discuss anything about them—or my past. Period."

Flustered, she said, "Don't be shy, Doc. Speak right up. Tell me what you *really* think."

"I just did."

"No kidding? Well, enough chitchat. It's almost eight. I'll have a passel of five-year-olds looking for me any minute." Backing toward the open door she felt behind her with one hand till she made solid contact with the jamb.

"Rachel…?"

There was a poignancy in his tone that would have

made her stop even if she hadn't been aware that she'd just jogged a tender spot in his memory. "Yes?"

"I'm sorry I came on so strong just now."

She smiled agreeably. "No problem. I have broad shoulders."

Sean returned her smile. "You're so tiny you barely have any shoulders at all. Maybe that's why I was so surprised when you told me you owned power tools. Is the offer still good? Can I come get a window or two and maybe borrow a drill once I decide what I need?"

"Of course. Just give me a call ahead of time to make sure I'm home. You know where I live. The number's in the book."

"I think I'll call Slocum's Garage and send my buddy Craig on a wild-goose chase, first," Sean joked. "He's not a real rational guy when he's around you."

"He never was. That's one of the reasons I decided not to marry him—no matter what."

"Whoa. I thought you said you weren't over him."

"It's a long story," Rachel said. "Actually, Craig did me a favor by breaking our engagement."

"How's that?"

"He helped me admit that I didn't need marriage to make me a complete person."

Given Rachel's undeniably maternal nature, Sean

was taken aback. "You really don't want a family? Kids of your own, I mean."

Waiting for an answer, he sensed her withdrawal. It didn't take a degree in psychology to see that she was shutting him out. Rachel Woodward might put on a good act most of the time, but there was definitely some unspoken outrage hidden beneath the persona she presented to the world. Whatever it was, it was bad enough to negate her normal good cheer. Of that, he was positive. He'd just watched it happen.

"You're starting to sound like my mother again," she said.

Sean carefully schooled his features, presenting a tranquil, amiable facade. "Tell you what. If you'll promise to stop mentioning my family, I'll try to avoid saying anything that reminds you of Martha. Okay?"

"Okay. Deal."

Rachel knew it was well past time to beat a hasty retreat. Whirling, she headed straight for the haven of her classroom. Sean had misunderstood her when he'd assumed she meant that he, personally, had reminded her of her mother. On the contrary. Being around him brought far different thoughts—thoughts that related directly to Martha's wish that her daughter would someday fall in love and marry.

That was one of the reasons why Rachel's conscience had twisted so uncomfortably when Sean mentioned having children. It was evident that having a family was high on his list of priorities, the same as it was on Craig's, which was a typical male trait. Women took on the care and nurturing of their children while men strutted around and bragged about what extraordinary kids they had produced.

"I'm happy single," she muttered to herself. "I like my life. I *love* my life. And I don't intend to complicate it by falling in love with anybody."

In her heart, she heard one word echo silently. *Liar.*

With so many students to look after and teach, Rachel wasn't surprised that the rest of the day seemed to pass quickly. When the dismissal bell rang, however, she realized how exhausted she was. It was definitely quitting time.

Samantha lagged back, remaining with her teacher instead of boarding the bus immediately. She gave Rachel's skirt a quick tug to gain her attention. "Can I come play with Schatzy today?"

"Today? I don't know. It's awfully hot again."

"I don't care. I don't have to take that old bus. I could go home with you."

Rachel already knew she'd made a grave mistake by inviting the little girl to visit in the first place. Yet when Samantha raised those big blue eyes and gave her such a needy look, she couldn't bear to refuse without offering a possible alternative.

"I can't take you home with me, Samantha. It's against the school rules. You have to ride the bus. I suppose it would be all right if Mrs. Brody wants to bring you over later, after I get home, though.''

The little girl was bouncing up and down like a doll suspended from rubber bands. ''Yeah!''

''But...if she decides she's too busy tonight, I don't want you to make a fuss. Understand?''

''*You* tell her. She'll do it if you tell her to.''

''We *ask* when we want someone to do us a favor,'' Rachel instructed gently. ''We don't tell them what to do. That isn't polite.''

''But you can make her do it,'' Samantha argued. ''You can make anybody do anything.''

Rachel laughed. ''I think you give me too much credit, honey. I don't have any special powers of persuasion.''

''Yes, you do. Angels can do lots of things. I saw them.''

Crouching beside her so she could look her straight in the eyes, Rachel asked, ''What did you see?''

''Angels. I told you.''

''When?''

Expecting the child to mention the classroom incident involving the weeping boy, Rachel was shocked when Samantha said, ''When my mommy and daddy went to heaven.''

Rachel had done her best to control her astonishment at Samantha's declaration about encountering angels. Nevertheless, she knew she'd reacted too strongly because the child had refused to explain further, even when she'd probed for details.

As soon as bus five pulled out, Rachel went in search of Sean. She found him coming out of his office. "Hi."

"Hi. What's up?"

Rachel stepped closer so they could converse privately, even though the hallway was now nearly deserted. "I think I just made a big mistake."

"You? A mistake? Perish the thought."

She playfully punched him in the shoulder. "Knock off the jokes, Bates. I'm trying to be serious here."

"Sorry. What's the problem?"

"It's Samantha."

"Don't tell me she took the wrong bus again."

"No. I made sure she got on number five and stayed there. It's something she said while we were out front waiting. She told me she'd seen angels—when her parents died."

"Go on."

"That's all I could get out of her," Rachel said with a sigh. "The minute I started asking questions, she clammed up. I thought maybe you could give me some pointers about what to say the next time she brings up the subject."

Sean pressed his lips together, his brows arching. "That's a tough one. It's not the kind of thing you can rehearse ahead of time. You just have to feel your way along. Were you careful to allow her to express herself without condemnation?''

''I hope so. I was trying to act nonchalant. I know I did fine until she mentioned her folks. After that, I'm not so sure. I couldn't believe how matter-of-fact she sounded.''

''Children are like that,'' Sean said. ''They accept death a lot easier than adults do. Samantha may have imagined angels were involved to help cushion the loss.''

''Maybe. Maybe not.'' Rachel's voice was barely a whisper.

Head cocked to one side, Sean leaned closer and strained to hear. ''What?''

''Never mind. I was just talking to myself,'' Rachel said. She couldn't help noticing how his nearness was speeding up her heartbeat and taking her breath away. It was bad enough that the afternoon humidity was stifling. Now, her emotions were kicking into high gear, too. The combination made her dizzy.

Sean touched her arm. ''You okay?''

''I don't care for the heat, that's all.''

''A fine Native American you make,'' he teased. ''Come on. I'll walk you back to your classroom.''

''That's not necessary.''

''I know it isn't. But how are we going to generate enough gossip to keep everybody occupied if we don't give them fresh news to pass around from time to time? We wouldn't want them to get bored.''

She gave a wry chuckle. "Perish the thought."

His grasp on her arm was firm and gentle—more than a caress but less than forceful. There was an unexplainable assuredness to it that gave Rachel moral as well as physical support. Perhaps friendship between them wasn't out of the question, even though he had overstepped its bounds when he'd caught her by surprise and kissed her.

Remembering that precious moment didn't help Rachel's dizziness one bit. Neither did the touch of Sean's strong hand on her bare arm. Heat or no heat, she wished she'd kept her jacket on instead of leaving the classroom in only her sleeveless cotton dress. The sheath was appropriate for summer wear, it simply didn't cover her upper arms enough to keep his hand from making direct contact with her skin.

They reached her classroom quickly. Sean ordered her to sit down while he fetched her a cup of water. "Drink."

"Let me sip it, okay?"

"Okay. I didn't see you in the staff room at lunchtime, today. Did you eat?"

"I needed to get art supplies ready for the afternoon lesson, so I ate a bite in here, while the kids were gone."

"A bite? Or a real lunch?"

"Well…"

"That's what I thought. No wonder you're woozy. Probably have low blood sugar. You didn't take nearly enough at Linden's the other day to get your money's worth, either.''

''I happen to love salads.''

''You still didn't eat enough to keep a rabbit alive.''

''I'm not a rabbit.''

One eyebrow arched and he grinned. ''No kidding. If I'd had teachers who looked like you when I was a kid, I might have done better in school.''

That confession surprised her. After taking a few sips of water she asked, ''You weren't a good student?''

''Not at first. It took me till I was out of high school to figure out that the only way I was ever going to make it on my own was to improve my education. Even then, I didn't go about it right.''

Rachel finished the cup of water and held it out to him with a smile and a ''Please?'' While he was re-filling it at the classroom sink, she questioned him further. ''What did you do wrong?''

''I didn't follow my heart. My brothers had ma-jored in business so I did the same. That was my first mistake. The second was trying to work with them. We fought all the time about how the store should be run. It wasn't until I was totally fed up that I realized I was a big part of the problem.''

''Because you weren't doing what you really wanted to do?''

''Exactly.'' Smiling, Sean handed her the refilled

cup. "How did you get so smart? I thought I was the psychologist around here."

"Horse sense." When he looked puzzled she amended her comment. "You know, plain old common sense."

"Right. The moment I met you I sensed you had intuitive capabilities. That's one reason I doubt you said or did anything to make Samantha wary of confiding in you. I suspect she'll come around and tell you the whole story when she's ready. In the meantime, she's been assigned as one of my first cases."

"That's wonderful. I'm so glad you're working here. I don't know how many times I've wished for a professional opinion about a student and had to muddle through myself, instead. I'll feel much better knowing I'm not struggling with Samantha's problems alone."

"Good. Happy to help." Sean took a backward step toward the door. "Well, I'd better be getting back to my office. Our esteemed boss was supposed to drop in after four and look over what I've done with the place. Not that that overgrown closet gives me much opportunity to be creative. I do still want to make one of those fake windows, though. Okay if I stop by your place on my way home today and pick one up?"

"No problem. I'm always home by five. If you get there ahead of me, just help yourself."

"And be shot as a trespasser by one of your gun-toting neighbors? No, thanks. If I don't see your car, I'll just park out front and wait for you.''

So much for avoiding him by dragging my feet, she thought ruefully. It figured. The way the past few weeks had been going, she was liable to wind up with a house full of guests this evening when all she really wanted to do was kick off her shoes, grab a tall glass of iced tea, plop down in front of the air conditioner and veg out till bedtime.

Rachel sighed. ''Okay. You can come tonight as long as you don't make it too late. Once the sun sets I'm usually ready for bed.''

''I'll get there early. Wouldn't want to accidentally catch you in your jammies,'' he teased. ''I'll bet they're cute. Do they have bunny feet? No, I don't suppose they would in the summertime.''

Rachel's eyes widened, her cheeks suddenly aflame. This wasn't the first time her creative imagination had run amok and toyed with notions of intimacy where Sean Bates was concerned. Yes, she knew it was wrong. As a Christian she wasn't supposed to let her innermost thoughts amble in that direction. However, she was also human. Those two elements of her being weren't mutually exclusive, but they did sometimes clash. Like now.

Wresting control from her daydream and forcing herself back to reality, Rachel stood, chin up, shoulders square, spine straight. ''Don't worry. You're perfectly safe. I never get ready for bed until I'm sure I won't have any more company.''

Laughing, Sean started toward the classroom door. ''That's comforting. Well, see you later.''

He was almost out the door when she called after him, ''And I *don't* wear pajamas with bunny feet.''

Chapter Ten

Physical exertion had never left Rachel as weary as the mental calisthenics she'd been doing lately. Exhausted, she shed her dress and donned shorts and a tank top as soon as she arrived home, then wandered out onto the shaded front porch with Schatzy. It was always soothing to stroke the little dog and swing slowly back and forth in the old glider. As long as there was a breeze to fan her, Rachel much preferred being outdoors in the evening when the temperature started to drop a bit.

Sighing, she pushed her bare feet against the plank floor of the porch to set the glider in motion. Oh, how she wished it were that easy to smooth out her tumbling thoughts. No matter how often she told herself it was useless to reflect seriously on any man, let alone one she hardly knew, her mind refused to stop dwelling on Sean Bates. She'd relived every moment with him, every word he'd spoken, so many times it was becoming impossible to separate reality from wishful thinking.

Moreover, she continued to worry about Samantha. All children had fantasy lives. That was natural. The problem was deciding where normalcy stopped and obsession began. Once Sean began working with the little girl, she hoped they'd gain a better understanding of the situation.

And if not?

Thoughtful, Rachel petted the contented dog lying beside her on the padded swing seat. There was no easy answer to that question. The simplest fix, from an adult standpoint, would probably be to get Samantha to admit she'd made up the stories about seeing angels.

On the other hand, if they tried to take away that support system, no matter how far-fetched it was, without providing another, Samantha might falter. Except for seeing things that weren't there, she was doing pretty well. The last thing Rachel wanted to do was knock the emotional props out from under a child who had already been through so much.

Traffic on Old Sturkie Road was rare. Consequently, Rachel noticed Hannah Brody's van as soon as it turned the corner off Main and started up the street.

Weary, she sighed and scooped up Schatzy so he

wouldn't get excited and dash in front of the approaching vehicle. By the time Hannah pulled into her driveway, the little dog was wiggling all over with joy and Rachel was getting the underside of her chin licked. Smiling, she waved.

"Hi there."

Hannah rolled down the driver's window to lean out. "Evenin'. I tried to call and ask if this was all right. You must not o' heard your phone."

"I just got home a few minutes ago. I didn't notice any messages on my answering machine."

"Won't talk to them things," Hannah said flatly. "Real folks is bad enough. You don't answer your phone by four rings, I hang up."

Chuckling, Rachel paused on the lawn to appreciate the cool feel of the grass beneath her feet. "Well, you're here now so Samantha may as well stay to play a while."

"What about your supper?" Hannah asked. "You had time to eat a bite?"

"I'm fine. I don't get very hungry in hot weather, anyway. I'll grab a snack later."

"Okay. If you say so. How about I run down to the market and get us some ice cream?"

Rachel heard Samantha's shrill voice yell "Yeah!" from inside the van. The child's enthusiasm was contagious.

"That sounds great to me, too," Rachel said. "Why don't you leave your co-pilot here? We'll get some dishes out and set up a picnic on the porch while you're gone."

That said, she opened the rear sliding door of the van and helped the little girl climb down.

"Long as you promise not to tell that Heatherington woman," Hannah cautioned.

"I won't. I promise." Rachel took Samantha's hand, holding tight to both her and Schatzy to keep them safe while Hannah backed out into the street. Just then, a familiar black car turned off Main and headed their way.

Hannah stopped and leaned out of the van to shout at Rachel, "Looks like I'd best make it a double order. What flavors does he like?"

"How should *I* know?" Rachel retorted. "I barely know the man."

To her chagrin, Hannah laughed. It was a cackle of disbelief if Rachel had ever heard one.

Sean pulled into Rachel's driveway, parked and got out. As he came around the rear of the car, Rachel could see that he'd been home to change after work. Clad in faded blue jeans and a plain T-shirt he looked like an altogether different person. He still hadn't started wearing a baseball-type cap the way most of the local men did, but the rest of him certainly blended in well.

He waved. "Hello."

"Sean!" Samantha was jumping up and down. "You came, too. I knew you would!"

He darted a look in Rachel's direction and shrugged, silently denying any collusion on his part. When Samantha barreled up to him, he caught her and swung her off the ground.

"Hi. How's my best girl?"

The child giggled. "She's fine. Me, too."

"I meant you, you little stinker," he said fondly. "Stop trying to get me in trouble with your teacher."

"Angels never get in trouble," Samantha told him in a stage whisper that could easily be heard all the way to where Rachel stood.

"I've been meaning to talk you about that," Sean said. "What makes you think I'm an angel?"

"'Cause you're nice. And you help people. Just like on TV."

"I see." Sean was beginning to feel a lot better about the child's fantasies. "You mean the program where the angels look just like regular people?"

"Uh-huh."

With a nod and a satisfied sigh, Sean put Samantha down. "Good. You go play now. I need to talk to your teacher."

The eager little girl wasn't about to be distracted. She circled him. "Can I see your wings? Please?"

"I don't have any wings," Sean said.

"But you can still fly, can't you?"

"Sorry. I can't do that, either."

"Not even float? Not even a little?"

"Nope. I'm afraid not."

"Bummer," the child murmured, pouting.

Watching the interplay between the handsome man and exuberant child, Rachel had covered her mouth to hide her smile. Now, she pressed her fingertips to her lips to keep from bursting into giggles.

As soon as Samantha dashed onto the porch in pursuit of her canine playmate, Rachel glanced up at Sean. There was so much merriment in his eyes and on his face, she had to chuckle in spite of her best efforts to contain herself.

"You sure you don't have wings?" she teased.

"Positive. Do you?"

"Not the last time I looked."

He made a silly pout reminiscent of Samantha's, lowered his already deep voice and said, "Bummer."

That was the last straw. Rachel erupted into laughter. By the time she finally regained control of herself there were tears rolling down her cheeks. She dashed them away. "I'm sorry. I tried not to lose it but..."

Sean was chuckling, too. "I know what you mean. I can see her mistaking you for an angel, but I sure can't picture myself that way."

"Thanks—I think."

"You're welcome." Continuing to laugh softly he looked toward the porch where Samantha was playing tug-of-war with the low-slung dog. "Has she asked to see your wings, yet?"

"No." Rachel sobered. "Has she told you any more about seeing angels right after her parents were killed?"

"I haven't broached the subject. I've just let her talk about whatever she wants to, and that hasn't come up."

"Probably because she figures all us angels already know everything," Rachel offered. "Do you think it would hurt if I came right out and asked her for details?"

"It might. Give her time. She'll discuss it more when she's ready."

Sighing, Rachel gazed with fondness at the lovely blond five-year-old. "I wish we knew more about the circumstances behind this obsession she has with angels."

I don't think there's anything to worry about," Sean said. "She apparently got the idea from watching TV. The concept fit her current life, so she used it—that's all."

"Uh-uh." Rachel shook her head slowly, pensive. "It's more than that."

"Now who's imagining things?"

Instead of answering directly, she asked a question. "What about you? Do you believe in angels?"

"In the supernatural, you mean?"

"If that's how you want to put it."

"Not really," he said with a shake of his head. "I believe in what I can see and touch."

"So you've told me. Have you given any thought to what we talked about right after Craig decked you?"

He unconsciously stroked his jaw. "Ducking faster?"

"No, silly. Things that are unseen, like faith and…" She hesitated, reluctant to mention love again.

Sean had no such qualms. "And love? I remember exactly what you said. It made an interesting analogy, but I have to disagree with your conclusions. Too unscientific."

"I suppose you still believe the world is flat, too."

He laughed. "No. I have it on good authority that the earth is relatively round, as long as you allow for the effect of the moon's gravity as it passes over."

"Gravity?" Rachel folded her arms across her chest and took a firm stance, her eyebrows raised. "How interesting. And just when did you see and touch *that?*"

"I don't have to see it to observe its effects," he argued.

"Exactly. The same goes for faith."

"Not hardly. Since we aren't floating off into space, I have all the proof of gravity I need."

Rachel smiled. "Has anybody ever told you you're as stubborn as a mule?"

"Often. Your point is?"

"Nothing. I give up. I should have known better

than to get into a theological debate with you. It's not up to me to convince you of anything. Whatever finally happens is between you and the good Lord. I have enough to worry about in my own life." She glanced toward the porch. "That little girl's future, for instance."

Sean had been feeling strangely uneasy with their former subject and was glad for the change of focus. "What do you think will happen to her?"

"I don't know." Careful to keep their conversation private, Rachel stepped closer to him to continue. "Health and Human Services says she has some shirt-tail relatives living somewhere up in Colorado. Hannah's convinced they weren't very keen to add to their family when they were told about Samantha. If no one else steps forward to lay claim to her, I assume she'll be put up for adoption. I just don't know how soon."

After a moment of silence broken only by the songs of birds and the cooing of Samantha as she cuddled Schatzy, Sean asked, "How about you? Why don't you consider adopting her?"

The idea wasn't new to Rachel. Neither was her decision. "I've thought about that. It's impossible."

"Why?"

"Because I don't have a proper home to offer her."

He swept his arm in an arc that took in her house and yard. The place was small and quaint, yet more of a home than a lot of children had. "Looks to me like you do. What's the real problem?"

"It's me, okay," she replied, irritated by his probing. "I'm not mother material, and I certainly don't intend to rob that poor little thing of the chance to belong to a complete family. Enough of my students have only one parent. There's no need to add another child who's forced to grow up that way."

"Humph. Funny," Sean said dryly. "I would have thought any permanent arrangement would be preferable to being passed from foster home to foster home the way Sam has been."

"Now you're doing it, too. Stop calling her *Sam*. Her name is Samantha. If you and Hannah had your way you'd have her sounding like a boy."

"Okay, okay." Sean held up both hands in surrender. "I stand corrected. Don't try to change the subject. I can buy the notion that two parents are preferable to only one, but one is certainly better than none. What I don't get is why you say you wouldn't make a good mother." He smiled mischievously. "Except for a stubborn streak and some nutty ideas about destiny, you seem like a perfect candidate for motherhood. What makes you think you're not?"

Rachel was not about to bare her innermost secrets to anyone, let alone a man she hardly knew. Telling Craig the whole truth had been necessary because of their plans to marry. It had also been the hardest thing she'd ever had to do. She wasn't up to repeating that crushing episode, especially since there was no need to reveal her physical shortcomings to Sean—or to anyone else for that matter.

Maybe someday, when she was older and hopefully wiser, she'd get around to telling her mother about the specialist who had warned her that she would never be able to conceive, never produce a family.

And maybe not. Lately, Martha had been so outspoken about the whole subject that Rachel had decided to keep her own counsel. That was certainly better than having her eager mother drag her to every fertility doctor from Little Rock to Springfield—or beyond.

"Look," she said flatly, "if the Lord wants me to have kids of my own, I'll have them, okay?" *Sure, if a miracle happens.* "Until then, I wish you'd stop needling me."

"Me?" Sean looked abashed. "Hey. I wasn't trying to bug you. I was just making a suggestion—and a pretty good one, too, if you ask me."

"That's the problem. I didn't ask you."

"Right." He stiffened, squared his shoulders. "Well, I didn't come here to bother you, Ms. Woodward. I came to look at those old windows you offered me. I'll pick one out and be on my way before I stick my foot in my mouth again."

His sudden shift to formality took Rachel by surprise. Had she really been that offensive? Apparently.

"Look, Sean, I'm sorry if I snapped at you. I guess I have a little hangup where my future is concerned."

"A *little* one?" He chuckled. "Lady, that's the understatement of the year."

"I wouldn't go that far."

"Okay. I don't want to argue. Your quirks are none of my concern. But what happens to Samantha Smith is. I just made the mistake of assuming you cared, too."

Before Rachel could recover from the shock of his comment and tell him how off base he was, he'd whirled and was headed toward her backyard, presumably in search of the old window he'd come for.

Pausing before following him, she called to Samantha and Schatzy. "Let's go, you two. Into the backyard. I don't want you playing out here all by yourselves."

The dog responded immediately, tail wagging and tongue lolling. The child, however, lagged back with a scowl and a plaintive "Awww."

"Now," Rachel ordered. "We'll be close enough to hear Mrs. Brody's van when she comes back. You won't miss your ice cream."

That explanation seemed to satisfy. Samantha skipped across the lawn to join Rachel, grasped her hand and tugged for attention.

When Rachel leaned down to listen, the little girl whispered, "You could show me *your* wings. I won't tell. I know I'm not supposed to."

Amused, Rachel played along with the fantasy. "Who told you not to tell?"

"The big angel who came to get me," Samantha said soberly. "He said not to be scared and not to tell anybody."

"A big angel? Like Mr. Bates?"

"Oh, no. Much bigger." She stretched out her free arm as far as it would go. "Bigger than this, even. He went way up to the sky."

"He did?" Pausing, Rachel bent down to look into the child's eyes. "What did he look like?"

"White, sort of. It was hard to see."

"Why was that?"

"'Cause he was so bright. Like the sunshine, only more. And he was strong, too."

"Very strong?" Awed, Rachel sensed that something profound was about to be revealed. She only hoped she could remain calm enough to listen without distracting the child.

Samantha nodded gravely. "*Real* strong."

Trying to keep from showing excess interest, Rachel fought to control her uneven breathing and willed her racing heart to slow down as she asked, "How do you know he was so strong?"

"You know, silly. 'Cause he picked up the car." A smile appeared briefly on her innocent face, then faded. "I told him to get Mommy and Daddy out, too, but he said they had to go to heaven."

"Oh, honey." Rachel opened her arms and pulled

the child into a tight hug. She'd read a brief history in Samantha's file. It hadn't been specific about how the Smiths had died, only that they'd perished together, leaving one daughter. "I didn't know you were with your mommy and daddy that day. You were all in a car accident? Is that what happened?"

The small blond head nodded against Rachel's shoulder.

"And you think an angel rescued you?"

"He did. Honest." She leaned back just enough to look at her teacher's face. "He was real nice. Like you."

Blinking back unshed tears, Rachel gave the child a kiss on her soft cheek. "Thank you, Samantha. That's the nicest thing anybody has ever said to me."

Chapter Eleven

Rachel and Samantha found Sean rummaging through the odds and ends of building materials, old and new, piled behind her storage shed.

"Watch out for spiders and snakes," Rachel warned, taking care to hold tight to the child to keep her out of danger.

He stepped back and dusted off his hands. "Wasn't that a popular song back in the early seventies?"

"How would I know? That was before my time." She grinned. "I'm not *old* like you are."

"Oh, fine. Stomp all over my ego. See if I care."

"I wasn't kidding about the danger, Sean. There are undoubtedly Black Widows and Brown Recluse spiders in that pile. As for the snakes, they'll probably run away unless they feel cornered."

"Thanks for the warning."

"You're welcome. We're about to share some ice cream out on the front porch. When you get finished back here, why don't you join us?"

"And risk getting my nose broken if Craig cruises by again?"

"Hannah will be here, too," Rachel explained with a light laugh. "There should be safety in numbers."

"Well, in that case, maybe I will. I am hungry. Haven't had my—" he pointedly glanced at his watch "—*supper,* yet."

"Good. I see you have learned a few things since you've been here. I haven't eaten either, but right now I'm more concerned with being cool than with good nutrition. Ice cream sounds heavenly. And speaking of Heaven, that reminds me," she lowered her voice till she was almost whispering, "I need to have a private talk with you."

Sean immediately glanced at the little girl by her side, and when he looked back at Rachel, she nodded. "I see," he said. "Okay. I'll put one of these windows in my trunk and meet you out front as soon as I can find a hose to rinse off my hands."

"Don't be silly. Go inside and wash in the kitchen or the bathroom," Rachel said.

"What about your reputation?"

"Humph," she snorted with disgust. "I'm afraid it's too late to worry about that."

"Why? What's wrong now?"

"Look over your shoulder."

Turning, Sean thought he saw quick movement in a window of the house next door. He blinked, frowned. "Who's that?"

"Miss Verleen," Rachel said. "She's a veritable fountain of knowledge. Anything you want to know, she can tell you. And more. Of course, half of it's supposition, but nobody cares about that. All they want is the gossip. Verleen's a master."

"Did you know that when you moved in here?"

"Oh, sure. I wasn't worried. I've always led a straightforward, honorable life." Rachel gave him a wry smile and chuckled softly. "Until I met *you,* I hadn't given her one single reason to talk about me."

"We didn't do anything wrong."

"Not wrong. Just interesting." The expression on his face made her laugh again. "Don't look so surprised."

"I know, I know. You warned me." He was shaking his head. "It's just hard to get used to being around anybody who cares that much one way or the other. Back home, I knew some of my neighbors, sure, but I guess my life was too hectic to spare much time wondering about what they were up to in their private lives."

"They were probably up to plenty," Rachel offered. "You just didn't know it."

"I suppose you're right. People will be people, wherever you go." With a wry grin he looked her up and down, clearly admiring her slim, petite self, then said, "Some of them are just a whole lot prettier than others."

By the time Hannah arrived with the promised ice cream, Rachel and Samantha were waiting on the porch. Sean came out the front door as the older woman was climbing the steps. She had a plastic sack in one hand and was using the other to pull herself up the stairs.

"Here," he said, reaching out, "let me help you with that."

"Ain't heavy," Hannah countered. She raised an eyebrow at Rachel, then glanced pointedly at the screen door.

"Sean was inside washing up," Rachel said. "He got dirty out back, and I didn't see any reason for him to have to wash his hands in the garden hose." Chin jutting out, she faced Hannah. "Do *you?*"

"'Course not. Well, where do you want me to put this?"

Samantha shouted, "Here!" holding out an empty blue plastic bowl. That made all the adults laugh. Even Hannah.

"Over here," Rachel said. "I moved my plants off this table. And here's a scoop and more bowls and spoons." While Hannah emptied her shopping bag, Rachel added, "I think you should dish up Samantha's first, before she busts a puckering string."

"Good idea. You wanna do it?"

"No. Go ahead. I'll be right back. I need to speak with Sean for a minute." The quizzical look on Hannah's face made her add, "About a certain little mutual friend."

To Rachel's relief, the other woman gave a sage nod. "You go right ahead, then. Sam and me, we'll start without you. Come get yourselves a dish when you're ready."

Sean was standing apart from the group, waiting. Rachel led him to the far end of the porch and stopped with her back against the railing so she could watch the child as she spoke and make sure they weren't being overheard.

"I found out more," she said softly.

"Go on."

He stepped aside and lounged against the front of the house, forming a right angle with Rachel so he could glance sidelong at the ice-cream party without being too obvious.

"There was a car accident. She was with her parents when they died."

"You're sure?"

"That's what she said."

"What else?" Sean asked, studying the giggling little girl.

"She told me an angel rescued her."

His head snapped around. "How?"

"Supposedly, this angel lifted the whole car off her and helped her escape."

Sighing pensively, Sean nodded. "It's possible someone came along and did that. There have been recorded instances of bystanders performing feats of enormous strength in times of stress. If a person saw a trapped child he might find it in him to pick up a vehicle."

"That's what you think happened?"

"Of course. What else could it be?"

"A real angel."

"Oh, come on, Rachel. You don't honestly believe in all that hocus-pocus, do you?"

"Why not?" She huffed cynically. "Oh, that's right. I forgot. You don't believe in anything you can't see or touch."

"You make it sound like I'm the one who's delusional."

"Aren't you?" Waving her hands in front of her she quickly added, "Never mind. Forget I said that." A smile raised the corners of her mouth. "It's not your fault. You can't help being blind to the miracles all around you."

"Nice of you to give me the benefit of the doubt."

"Not at all. I sometimes forget that not everyone sees life the way I do. Think of yourself as a lamp with a cord that's not plugged in. You can try to turn that lamp on all you want, but it'll never give light unless it's properly connected."

"Are you calling me a dim bulb?" Sean gibed.

"Oh, no. I think you're one of the brightest people I've ever known."

"Thanks." His gaze narrowed on her, obviously saw the twinkle of mischief in her eyes. "Okay. What's the catch?"

"No catch. I just hope I'm there when you finally discover all you've been missing."

Sean chuckled to himself. "I don't—not that I'm agreeing with you, mind you."

"Why not? You chicken?"

"No. I just hate to be wrong. Once I've made up my mind, it's not in my nature to change it."

"Then, you and I are in for a lot of trouble," Rachel quipped, "because I never back down, either."

"Never?" He pushed off the wall where he'd been leaning and took one step closer to her, then another.

"Well, *almost* never," Rachel said, finding herself suddenly trapped.

Ducking to dodge around him she hurried back to where Samantha was shoveling in ice cream while also entertaining Hannah with stories of previous ice-cream treats.

Rachel grinned at them, hoping she wasn't blushing from her close encounter with Sean. "Well, here I am. What's good? Or should I ask, what's left?"

"I got strawberry!" the little girl announced. "It's larupin'."

"That good, huh?" She laughed, looking to Hannah. "Have you been teaching Samantha new expressions?"

"Maybe a few. She does learn real fast, that's a fact. Be a shame to lose her."

Rachel had the scoop in her hand and was filling it with rapidly softening ice cream. She stopped abruptly. "Lose her? Why? I thought everything was okay."

"So'd I, till this afternoon. I got a call from a lady up north in Colorado, Sam's aunt, by marriage, on her papa's side. She's thinkin' 'o steppin' in, after all."

"What? Those people weren't interested before. Why the change? And why *now?*"

"I think there's an inheritance," Hannah said, turning aside and lowering her voice. "Don't know how big, not that it matters to me. Doesn't take much money to win over some folks, though."

"That's terrible! We can't let—"

Coming up behind Rachel, Sean interrupted by laying his hand gently on her shoulder and saying, "I'm sure we all want whatever's best for Samantha."

When Rachel turned to look up at him, she couldn't help her unshed tears.

He relieved her of the ice-cream scoop and stepped up to take her place. "You having strawberry, Miss Rachel?"

"Um…yes."

"I see there's chocolate, too. I think I'll have some

of that." With a polite smile he went on to ask, "Mrs. Brody? Can I get you something?"

"I'm fine, thanks. Already had a bite of each. But help yourself to all you'd like. It's fixin' to melt, anyway."

"I think it already has melted," Sean said. "I like it that way, myself. How about you, Samantha? Would you like more?"

She held out her half-empty dish. "Yes, please. I want chocolate, like you."

"Would you like it in a separate bowl?"

The child looked puzzled. "Why?"

"No reason," he said with a short laugh. "I was just remembering how my brother Ian used to eat everything. He didn't want any flavors mixed together."

"Oh." Studying the softening scoops in her bowl when Sean handed it back, Samantha paused a moment, then gave the whole thing a quick stir with her spoon and held it up for him to see. "Look! I made a picture!"

"Hey, great."

"Know what it is?" she asked.

Sean glanced over at Rachel, as if hoping for rescue, but she was still fighting back her tears.

"Let me think," he drawled, stalling. "It kind of looks like—um—an angel?"

Samantha giggled behind her hand. "No, silly! It's Schatzy. See? It has a red collar and everything."

"Actually, it looks more like a glob of melted ice

cream than anything else,'' Sean countered, laughing with her. "I think you're teasing me."

That sent the child into a fit of giggles. The laughter was so contagious that even Rachel had to smile. She nodded to Sean. "I think you're right."

"Samantha has a wonderful imagination," he told Rachel. "Remember that when you're talking to her. Know what I mean?"

"I know exactly what you mean." She picked up the dish of strawberry he'd fixed for her and tasted a spoonful, savoring the cool, smooth sweetness before she went on. "I also know what I believe. See that you don't forget that, either."

"Are you likely to let me?" he asked, muting a wry grin and trying to look more serious than he felt.

"Not in a million years, mister."

Sean nodded and smiled amiably, including everyone in the magnanimous gesture. "Good. I wouldn't know what to do with myself if you quit picking on me."

Rachel's eyes widened. "Picking on you? Me? I've been trying to *help* you!"

If Sean had been the only one to laugh, Rachel wouldn't have been surprised. However, when Hannah also began to guffaw, Rachel's brow wrinkled with confusion. "What's so funny?"

"You two are," the middle-aged woman said. "The way you argue sounds just like me and my Hank used to, back when we started courtin'."

* * *

Rachel didn't mind Sean lingering after the others left. Truth to tell, she needed another adult to talk to. Preferably someone *other* than her mother.

When she started to carry the dirty bowls into the house, Sean pitched in and followed. "I'll bring what's left of the ice cream. I'm pretty sure it's not salvageable, though."

"There isn't much. You can dump it in the sink. Just don't let it drip on the carpet on the way to the kitchen."

"Can't we feed it to the animals?"

"Not the chocolate. It's toxic to dogs and cats."

"I didn't know that."

Rachel smiled at him over her shoulder. "See? Stick with me and you'll learn something new every day."

"Is that a guarantee?" he asked, amused.

"Close to it. I was planning to tutor you in country ways, remember?"

"How could I forget?"

Rachel laughed softly, enjoying his wry humor. Then she sobered. "You can do me a favor in return."

"Sure. Name it."

She set the bowls in the sink beside the cardboard ice-cream containers he'd put down, and rinsed off her sticky fingers before turning to look up at him. "I want you to get a copy of the police report on the death of Samantha's parents."

"Why? What good will that do?"

"Maybe none." Pensive, Rachel dried her hands on a kitchen towel. "Then again, maybe the report will give us a better idea of how best to approach her."

"Okay, I'll do what I can. It might take some time."

"According to Hannah, time is one thing we may not have a lot of," Rachel countered. "Look, Sean, I know I'm no expert like you are, but even I can see that Samantha's got some king-size hang-ups. Who wouldn't? Especially since she saw the whole horrible accident."

"If she really did," he replied. "It's also possible that she imagined being there."

"Why would she do that?"

"Maybe because she subconsciously felt she should have been hurt, too. Or maybe because she thinks she could have saved everybody if she'd been with them."

"What about the angel story? Do you really think she imagined all that?"

"Probably. The mind plays funny tricks under extreme stress." He reached for Rachel's hand, meaning only to offer consolation, but the instant he touched her he knew it was more than that. Much more. An undeniable current flowed between them, connecting them in some intangible way.

She grasped his hand in both of hers and held firm,

looking up at him with misty, pleading eyes. "I want to help her, Sean. I have to. It's like she was *sent* here to me. Can you understand that?"

Understand? Did he? From an intellectual standpoint, yes. From an emotional one, however, he had to admit he didn't have a clue. If he were to concede that there might be a Higher Power at work in anyone's life, he'd also have to acknowledge that the same Power could be affecting him. That concept was ridiculous, of course. Man was in charge of his own destiny. He, of all people, knew that. After all, he'd been just as apt as the rest of his family to lean on alcohol as an easy escape from reality, yet he'd managed to thwart those inherent tendencies. So far.

"It doesn't matter what I do or don't believe," Sean said. "It's what you think that counts. If you want my assistance in dealing with Samantha, I'll be more than happy to help—as long as it's in the best interests of the child."

"I'd never do anything that wasn't," Rachel insisted.

"Not willfully, no. The only thing that worries me is how attached you're getting to her already."

"She needs love. You can't tell me she doesn't."

"Of course she does. We all do." He felt Rachel's grip on his hand tighten and he laid his other hand over hers. "That doesn't mean you have to be more to her than her teacher."

Rachel knew he was right. She also realized it was

too late to lock up her heart and keep it from responding to such obvious need as Samantha's, nor would she want to. But what about Sean's needs. What about her own? When he'd told her that everybody needed love, she'd sensed that he was speaking more from a personal standpoint than an objective one. Clearly, he needed somebody to love him unconditionally.

Not me! she immediately countered. She already had her hands full looking after this year's class of five-year-olds and she didn't intend to take on the burden of worrying about a "lost" adult, too. Let him find his own answers, his own niche in life. Hers was already crammed with enough responsibilities to last a lifetime.

Oh, that was real Christian, Rachel, she told herself. *What a wonderful example you make. How proud Jesus must be of you!*

Ashamed of her selfish inclinations, she held tight to Sean's hands and boldly lifted her gaze to meet his. "I want to be Samantha's special friend," she said softly, earnestly. "And yours, too."

He didn't say anything in reply. He didn't have to. The gratitude and fondness in his expression spoke for him, leaving her so deeply touched that she wanted to open her arms and give him a hug of encouragement, of validation, the way she often did her emotionally needy students.

In Sean's case, she knew it wasn't very smart to consider putting her arms around him. It wasn't logical. But it was the right thing to do. And this was the right time.

Rachel didn't care if her nosy neighbors peeked through the windows, misinterpreted her actions and shouted about them from the rooftops. Sean Bates needed a hug and he was going to get one. Right now. From her. So there.

He looked a little surprised when she pulled her hands away, then responded instinctively when she slipped her arms around his waist and stepped into his embrace.

In any other context she might have fretted that her behavior would give him the wrong impression. At this moment, however, she was confident he understood.

Laying her cheek on his chest she held him close and listened to the steady beating of his heart. This was not the breathless, frantic embrace of two clandestine lovers. It was deeper. More poignant. Almost spiritual.

Rachel didn't know whether Sean was surprised or even if he was having the same kind of reaction to their closeness that she was. The only thing she was sure of was that she'd never felt this special, this safe, this *loved,* in her whole life.

Chapter Twelve

In retrospect, Rachel wasn't sure which one of them had made the first move to relax their embrace. She only knew that they had thought and acted as one, perfectly in tune. How very unusual. How awesome!

Stepping back, she tilted her head to look up at Sean's handsome face and was astonished to see traces of moisture in his eyes. Deeply affected, without pausing to consider the possible repercussions, she lifted her hand and tenderly, lovingly, cupped his cheek.

Sean placed his hand over hers, drew it around to his lips and kissed her palm.

Unsteady, Rachel laid her free hand on his chest and felt the pounding of his heart as it raced with her own runaway pulse. Her eyes closed. Her lips parted, trembled.

Lurking unheeded in the back of her mind was the caution that she should break away, should call a halt to what was happening.

She ignored the warning. Even her most vivid fantasies had never shown her this kind of belonging, this purity of devotion and endearment. Stop it? On the contrary—she wanted this wonderful moment to go on forever!

Sean slid his hand around the back of Rachel's neck and pushed his fingers through the silky thickness of her hair. Then he tilted his head and bent to kiss her.

She put her arms around his neck and raised on tiptoe to meet him boldly. This kiss began softly, cautiously, like the one on her front porch had, then quickly intensified until she lost all sense of reality. Instead of seeing the situation clearly, she imagined herself floating off into the clouds just like one of Samantha's angels.

It was Sean who finally tore himself away. He was breathing quickly and gawking at her as if he'd suddenly discovered a total stranger sharing his embrace.

Speechless, Rachel stared up at him. The tingle that had begun in her lips now included her entire being. Nothing seemed real except Sean. Nothing mattered but him. Being near him. Touching him. Trusting him completely. She wanted to ask him a thousand questions, yet her brain refused to cooperate and empower her voice. The loss of that much self-control was so frightening that it helped wake her up and bring her back down to earth—at least partially.

Could this be what it was like to fall in love? Rachel wondered. Or had she suddenly lost her mind? Given her usually levelheaded approach to life, she suspected the latter. A few seconds ago she had been so emotionally unstable she might have done something really stupid—and sinful—if Sean had asked.

Thank the Lord he hadn't! Which proved that Somebody Up There was still looking out for her, she reasoned, although she knew she would have been the one ultimately responsible if she'd lost control and stepped over the line. It was no use trying to shift the blame to God when free will was involved. Clearly, she must never let herself get into that kind of a situation again with any man.

Rachel drew a shaky breath as the truth hit her squarely in the heart. No other man had ever affected her the way Sean just had! None had even come close. Not even Craig Slocum, the man she'd once planned to marry. Following that line of logic, breaking up with Craig had been a blessing, not the disappointing loss she'd imagined it to be.

Her eyes widened. Her jaw gaped. She stared up at Sean, finally managing a squeaky "Oh-oh."

"Yeah. You can say that again."

His voice was rough, raspy. Looking flustered and embarrassed, he cleared his throat as he took a step backward. "I think I'd better be going."

All Rachel could do was nod. She followed him through the small house and out onto the front porch. It was one thing to know she shouldn't try to stop Sean from leaving and quite another to actually keep her mouth shut and let him go. What she really wanted to do was throw herself into his arms and beg him to stay, to hold her and kiss her again, to make her forget everything else.

Acting on that idiotic impulse was out of the question, of course. Seeing him every day at work was going to be difficult enough after this. Letting him know that she had developed a schoolgirl crush on him would make it a hundred times worse, especially since nothing positive or lasting could ever come of a relationship between them. To encourage him romantically would be more than foolish—it would be cruel.

Seeing him heading for his car reminded her of the original reason for his visit. She shaded her eyes against the brightness of the setting sun and called, ''Do you still want to borrow my hammer or my electric drill?''

Sean's laugh was coarse, self-deprecating. ''No, thanks. The way I'm feeling right now, redecorating is the last thing on my mind.''

It only took three working days for Sean to come up with the copy of the accident report that Rachel had requested.

He was thankful he'd managed to avoid running into her at school—probably with a lot of help from her—since their last ill-fated kiss in her kitchen. Now, however, in order to properly do his job, he was going to have to stop dodging her.

He contemplated slipping the report into her school mailbox rather than handing it over face-to-face. Delivering it like an interoffice memo would be a lot easier on him.

It would also be a cop-out, he reasoned, angry with himself for even considering such a thing. Taking care of the children he'd been assigned to was his sworn responsibility. If that meant he had to face the one woman who could tie his insides in knots with a mere smile, then so be it.

Had the report been faxed to the school earlier in the day, Sean could have passed it to Rachel at lunch or on her break. Unfortunately, he didn't receive the pages until well after three in the afternoon. That meant he had to let it wait till the following morning, try to catch Rachel before she went home or follow her to her house. That third option was out of the question. However, since their time to help Samantha was rapidly running out, waiting another day wasn't fair, either.

Which meant he'd better get a move on. He started looking for Rachel on the front lawn by the bus zone. She wasn't there. Hurrying to her classroom, he tried the door. It was locked. The lights were off.

Frustrated, he wheeled and jogged toward the one other place she might be—the faculty parking lot. Until he spotted her getting into her car, he hadn't realized how relieved he'd been when he'd thought he'd missed catching up to her.

He swallowed his pride and waved. "Rachel! Wait."

She paused and looked back, her hand on the door, one foot already inside the car. As Sean drew closer, she straightened and faced him.

"What's wrong?"

"Nothing. I just…" He waved the loose sheets of paper while he grabbed a few quick, extra breaths. "I knew you'd want to see this ASAP."

"What is it?"

"The police report you asked for. About Sam's parents."

Frowning and still gripping the open door, she eyed her car as if it were a lifeboat and the parking lot had suddenly become an ocean of hungry sharks. "You can see I'm on my way home. Why did you wait this long to bring it to me?"

"Had to," Sean said. "It just came."

"Oh." Rachel was chagrined. "Okay. I apologize. So, what does it say? Was Samantha in the car that day?"

"I don't know. Haven't taken the time to read it." He held out the papers. "I've been trying to find you ever since Mary told me this fax was here."

''Well,'' Rachel said with a sigh, ''come on, then. Let's go sit in the shade and read it together. Then we'll both know what it says and we can discuss it intelligently.''

''Sure.''

Only, Sean wasn't sure. Not about anything. The moment he'd sighted Rachel his heart had leapt into his throat and lodged there, cutting off half his air and leaving him thoroughly disconcerted. He knew it was impossible, yet every time he saw her she seemed prettier. More appealing. Sweeter. Each time he parted from her he'd be positive she could never improve on such absolute flawlessness. But she always did.

Falling into step behind her, he watched her graceful walk, noticed the way fine tendrils of hair had escaped from the pinned-up twist at the back of her head, saw how light her step was even though she had to be weary from a long day. He grimaced. It wasn't fair of her to look that good when he was trying so hard to do the right thing by staying away from her and not letting himself get involved.

Too late, his conscience insisted. *You're already more than involved. You're in love with her, you dummy. Now what are you going to do about it?*

Nothing, Sean countered firmly. A woman like Rachel needed a husband who came from a normal family, a man who wasn't afraid to become a father. Someone who could give her children without worrying about passing on the tendencies toward alcoholism and addiction that had polluted his lineage for generations.

And she also needed someone who fit into her world a lot better than he did, he decided easily. Judging by what he'd already observed, even if he did eventually find his niche in Serenity, he'd never be one of the "natives." That was a state of being a person was born into, not one that could be adopted.

Knowing he was right, Sean's heart ached. Some things were obviously meant to be. Others were not. It was bad enough that he'd kissed Rachel the first time. Repeating that mistake had been totally reckless. Idiotic. He'd let himself follow his heart's leading, and now he was stuck living with the consequences, the memories.

Sean sighed quietly. There was no way to undo the damage already done, but he could still protect Rachel. She'd be fine, as long as he never let on that he'd fallen head-over-heels in love with her.

Rachel led him into the shade of a broad oak and settled herself on one end of the bench beneath it.

Sean remained standing until she looked up at him quizzically and asked, "Why don't you sit down? You're making me nervous."

"Okay." With a purposely nonchalant shrug he took a seat as far from her as the bench would allow.

Leaning forward, he rested his elbows on his knees and laced his fingers together, ostensibly ignoring her.

If Rachel hadn't been so engrossed in the sketchy report she was reading, she'd have stopped right then to question Sean more. For the past few days he'd been acting ridiculous, dodging her as if she were some kind of predator and he were her prey!

The more she thought about it, the angrier she got. After all, she hadn't thrown herself at him. In both instances their kisses had been his idea, not hers. So how dare he avoid her as if everything that had happened between them was her fault?

The instant she finished scanning the report she thrust it toward him with a terse "Here."

He straightened and took it. "What's the matter? Didn't you find out what you wanted to know?"

"The report says Samantha was in the car, just like she told me she was. There's no mention of any good Samaritan lending a hand, like you thought."

"That doesn't mean there wasn't one."

"True."

Sean scowled over at her. "Why are you acting like you're mad at me? I didn't write the stupid report."

"The way I feel right now has nothing to do with that report," she countered. "It's you."

"Me? What did *I* do?"

"Nothing. Everything." Giving in to frustration, Rachel jumped up and began to pace in front of the bench. "You've been treating me like I have the plague."

"Me? You're the one who's been avoiding me!"

"I have not."

"What about the time you got up and left the lunchroom the minute I walked in?"

"I happened to be finished eating. But how about when you were coming out of your office yesterday and I was walking by? You turned around and ducked back in, the minute you saw me."

"I did not. I— I just left something on my desk and had to go back for it, that's all."

"Right. And pigs can fly."

Sean couldn't help smiling as he glanced at the sky and ducked for effect. "I sure hope not."

"It's not funny." Rachel was having trouble remaining irate in the face of his captivating grin.

"Yes, it is. Know what? You're really cute when you're upset."

"Upset? Who said I was upset?"

"Are you telling me you're not? Tsk-tsk. I think your halo is slipping, Ms. Woodward."

"If I have one, it's probably down around my ankles right about now," she countered wryly. "I told you Christians weren't perfect. I keep trying, though."

"If I wanted to keep you all riled up I'd tell you you're *very trying,* but since I've promised myself I'll behave when I'm around you, I won't say it."

"Oh, thanks. That makes me feel *much* better."

"I knew it would," Sean said with a laugh. "And you're right. I have been avoiding you. I thought it was best."

Rachel heaved a sigh and nodded. "Yeah. Me, too. I guess we're being silly. After all, we do have to work together. There's no way we can both occupy such a small campus and not accidentally run into each other."

"I suppose not."

She smiled. "The past few days have been interesting, though. I almost fell this morning when you popped out of your office and I ducked into the ladies' room to avoid you. The floor had just been mopped. For a few seconds there, I thought I was going to slide into the sinks, fall down and break my— neck."

"That sounds pretty drastic," Sean said, "and awfully hard to explain on an accident report. I suggest we both stop acting like kids with grudges and begin behaving like sensible adults."

Rachel pulled a face. "Aww. Do we have to?"

"I intend to try."

"Really? You aren't going to grab me and kiss me again?"

"I certainly hope not." He sobered. "I realize what a terrible mistake that was."

Chin raised, she defended her wounded pride with a terse "It certainly was."

"You hated it?" A muted smile gave away the fact he was teasing again.

"Worst kiss I ever had," she replied.

"Liar. There goes your halo again."

Rachel made a derisive noise and scrunched one corner of her mouth into an exaggerated jeer. "Halo? Ha! As long as I hang around you, I'll probably never even come close to earning one."

"And you blame me for that? Oh, great. Now I suppose I'm responsible for keeping you out of heaven, too?"

"It doesn't work like that." She paused to give him an encouraging pat on the arm, leaving her hand there just a fraction too long before she came to her senses and jerked it away. "I don't believe people can ever be good enough to earn their way into Paradise. I know I certainly couldn't. That's where Jesus comes in."

"He has your admission ticket, you mean?"

Rachel smiled sweetly and said, "Yes. He's got everybody's. Even yours. Bought and paid for."

"I sincerely doubt that."

"I know you do. That's too bad."

"Why? Because you can't talk me into buying your belief system?"

"No, because I like you, Sean. I don't want to see you miss out on all the blessings the Lord has waiting for you."

"Yeah, well, my folks went to church all the time

and it never did them much good that I could see. The only time I ever heard my dad mention God was when he was drunk as a skunk and cursing at the top of his lungs.''

Once again she laid her hand on his arm, this time with more tenderness, greater courage. ''Try not to look at the worst examples. Even good Christians have bad days. We all make mistakes we regret later. The point is, we may be far from faultless but we're learning how to live better lives all the time. That's why I go to church. Think of it as God's School.''

''I'd probably flunk out.''

''Why? Because your father did?'' She ignored the disgusted glance he gave her and went on. ''Have you ever asked yourself what he might have been like without his faith?''

Sean huffed. ''Don't even go there.''

''Why not?''

''Because, thanks to my brothers, I already know. I've watched Paul and Ian all my life. It hasn't been pretty.''

''That doesn't mean you're the same kind of person they are,'' Rachel insisted.

''Doesn't it? Tell that to a geneticist and see what he says.''

''I'd rather trust the Lord than rely on scientists. Oh, they have their place. I'm not saying they don't. But they can claim to have all the right answers one day, then turn around and contradict themselves the next. The more they learn, the more they realize they don't really know.''

Pausing, she began to smile in spite of the seriousness of their discussion. ''The same thing happens to me when I begin to study the Bible. I know I'll never understand everything about it. Fortunately, a person doesn't have to be well educated to become a Christian. Faith isn't reasoned. It's more basic than that.''

''How so?''

Rachel laughed at herself and shook her head. ''I wish I could explain. All I know is what happened to me after my father got sick.''

Sean was studying her expression. Empathetic, he reached for her hand. ''Go on.''

''I was barely a teenager at the time. Daddy and I were very close. I didn't see how I could live the rest of my life without him if he died. Thoughts of suicide kept popping into my head. That really scared me. Finally, when I thought I was at the end of my rope, I called out to Jesus. I don't know why I did it. I just know that at that moment, everything changed for me.''

Gently squeezing her fingers, Sean said, ''I'm glad your parents gave you a faith to call on when you needed it.''

''Did they?'' Rachel raised misty eyes to him and blinked back tears. ''When I went to them and tried to explain how happy and relieved I felt, they didn't seem to understand what I was trying to say. It wasn't until just before Daddy died that he told me he'd turned to Jesus the same way I had.''

''What about your mother?''

''Martha Woodward is already as perfect as any Christian can get. Ask her. She'll be more than happy to tell you.''

''So you're still worried about her?''

''Yes. And no. I did all I could when I told her about my conversion. I can't coerce her into believing, any more than I can convince you to give God a chance. If you choose not to open your mind to the spiritual possibilities all around you, then that's your choice. It always will be.''

Chapter Thirteen

Rachel didn't have to try to get away from Sean after she spoke so boldly. He seemed more than happy to part company with her.

Heading for home, she tried to relive their conversation, hoping to assure herself she hadn't been too preachy. Not only were most of her brilliant comments beyond recall, she couldn't even be sure she was putting the parts she did remember into the proper sequence. For all she knew, she might have alienated him for good, when that was the opposite of what she wanted to do.

That's what I get for praying for the guy. Thanks, Father. But I didn't mean I wanted to be the one to talk to him. I wanted You to send somebody else. Anybody but me. Please?

No booming voice came out of the clouds to answer, nor did Rachel expect it to. She'd had enough experiences with what she viewed as God's sense of humor to recognize an ongoing satire, especially when she was such an integral part of it. The temptation to try to figure out the Good Lord's plans beforehand was strong, as usual. It was also foolhardy. The more she tried to help, the more likely it was that everything would get worse. Quickly.

So what am I supposed to be doing? she prayed. *Just tell me and I'll do it, Father. I promise.*

Sweet thoughts of Sean were joined by the image of Samantha the first time Rachel saw her. Such a pitiful little thing. So lost. So in need of love. However much time they had left to get to know her, it wouldn't be half long enough.

The idea of some shirttail relative claiming that dear little child made Rachel's temples throb. It wasn't right. The law shouldn't be allowed to interfere and move her. Not when Samantha was finally getting settled, finally acting more like a normal, happy child.

"So, what am I doing going home when I could be headed for Hannah's, instead?" Rachel asked herself aloud.

That was such a good question that she turned right instead of left on Highway 62 and started toward Squirrel Hill Road.

In her heart she knew she was doing the right thing.

The peace of mind that immediately soothed her when she made her decision was further proof she was finally on the right track.

The Brodys were at home when Rachel pulled up in front of their old farmhouse.

Drying her hands on her apron, Hannah came out onto the porch. "Well, hello there. You missed supper, but I think I can scare up a bit more if you're still hungry."

"I don't want to be a bother. I can't stay. I was just on my way home and got this urge to stop by. Hope it's all right."

"'Course it is. You come right on in."

Climbing the front steps to the covered porch made Rachel feel as if she were returning to a beloved home. Hannah's house had been her refuge on more than one occasion, especially in the difficult months after her father's death. In retrospect, she supposed if she'd been older at the time she'd have been more tolerant of her mother's vacillating moods.

"Is Samantha busy?" Rachel asked.

"That child is always busy. Never sits still for more'n a minute or two." She gave a satisfied sigh. "Right now, I suspect she's out in the chicken house collectin' eggs for the third or fourth time today. Poor hens can't stay ahead of her."

Laughing softly, Rachel remembered doing the same chore for Hannah as a child. "That used to be a favorite job of mine, too. I swore I could tell those hens apart. Even had names for them.''

''I know. You used to say they talked to you, too. Always did have a wonderful imagination. I 'spect that's why you cotton to kids the way you do.''

''Which reminds me,'' Rachel said. ''Sean got me a copy of the accident report about Samantha's parents. She was in the car with them when they wrecked, just like she said. According to the investigator, she was thrown clear.''

Thoughtful, Hannah nodded. ''Could be.''

''Yes, it could, only she didn't have a scratch on her. The car was totaled. It rolled over and over, then landed upside down at the bottom of a ravine.''

''Maybe she fell out before it happened.''

''That was my first thought.'' Rachel raised her eyebrows and shook her head slowly as she explained further. ''Samantha was found at the bottom of the cliff right next to the flattened car. If she did fall out, it wasn't until the major damage had already been done. So why wasn't she hurt?''

''You thinkin' what I'm thinkin'?''

''That her guardian angel actually did rescue her?'' Rachel shrugged. ''I don't know. The report also said that it looked like her seat belt might have been cut to free her, which contradicts the theory that she was thrown clear. She's small. If she was wearing a belt and riding in the back seat, that might explain how she survived when the car was crushed, but it still doesn't explain how she managed to free herself while she was hanging upside down, then wiggle out without getting cut on broken glass or jagged pieces of metal.''

''Well, never you mind,'' the older woman said. ''What's done is done. Don't matter to me if she crawled out or if the good Lord pitched her out a window. Our little angel was spared and that's all that counts.''

''True.''

The sound of an approaching car caught their attention, bringing an ''Uh-oh'' from Rachel and, ''Well, well, well, looks like I got more company'' from Hannah Brody.

''I'd better be going.'' One quick look told Rachel the oncoming car was Sean's.

''Nonsense. You didn't drive clear out here just to tell me about the accident report, did ya? Don't you wanna see Sam, too?''

''Well, I did, but...''

''Then, don't go runnin' off just because *he's* here,'' Hannah cautioned. ''Hank and me'll protect you from him.''

Rachel huffed. ''Who's going to protect me from myself?''

As she'd expected, her candid comment made Hannah laugh.

''I 'spect I will,'' the older woman said. She opened the screen door and ushered Rachel inside.

"You go on out in the kitchen and make yourself at home. I'll send Mr. Bates to the chicken house to fetch Sam. That'll give you time to pull yourself together and act natural."

"Okay."

With a sigh of resignation Rachel made her way through the house to the old-fashioned farm kitchen. The room was the largest in the house, plenty big enough to cook for a slew of farmhands or set up a home-canning operation at harvesttime. Now that the need for that much extra space was long past, Hannah had replaced the wood cookstove with a modern range. The round stovepipe opening in the wall above it was capped but could still be seen, a reminder of the hard work previous generations of women had done on that very spot.

Finding the kitchen empty, Rachel gravitated to the rectangular table in one corner, took the same seat she'd often occupied as a child and unconsciously brushed her hands across the plastic tablecloth to smooth it. The lingering aroma of home cooking made the place seem even more appealing. Her stomach growled.

Hannah breezed in the back door with a broad smile. "Stay right where you are. I'm fixing to feed you."

"That's really not necessary," Rachel said. "I didn't come here to mooch a meal."

"Nonsense. Where'd my Southern hospitality be if

I didn't offer? Besides, your Mr. Bates has agreed to eat a bite with us, too.''

"He's not *my* Mr. Bates!" Eyes wide, Rachel peered past Hannah to see if Sean had followed her inside. Thankfully, he hadn't. "Where is he, anyway?"

"Outside, talkin' to Hank and Sam.'' Hannah began pulling plates and bowls of leftovers out of the refrigerator and placing them on the table. "You two sure coulda fooled me. Miz Slocum tells me her son's real upset over what's been goin' on.''

Rachel jumped to her feet. "Nothing's been going on!''

"Oh yeah? Then, why're you and Sean seein' so much of each other?''

"For Samantha's sake, of course.''

"Pooh.''

"Pooh, nothing. She's in my class and Sean's been assigned to counsel her. It's perfectly logical that he and I would want to compare notes—especially since you said there was a chance she'd be leaving here soon.''

Hannah reached out to pat Rachel's hand. "That's a fact. But don't you fret. There's lots 'o mixed-up kids these days. Once Sam's gone, I'm sure you can find another reason to keep seein' your new fella.''

"Ugh!'' Rachel was beside herself with frustration. "I meant what I said. There is *nothing* between me and Sean. Nothing. And I'm not fixin' to start anything. Okay?''

"Okay. Just remember, you aren't gettin' any younger. You'll have to settle down one day soon. Any man lucky enough to snag you will be the envy of every bachelor in town.''

"No, he won't." Somber, Rachel shook her head for emphasis. "I don't care what lies Craig told his mother, he was glad to be rid of me. That's why I don't understand what made him haul off and hit Sean the way he did.''

"Jealousy.''

"That's impossible," Rachel said. "Craig doesn't want me.''

"You sound like you think nobody does. So you had a problem with Craig. So what? He's not the only deer in the forest, you know. You'll find somebody else.''

"I don't *want* to find anyone else. That's what I keep trying to tell my mother. I'm never getting married. Period.''

Confused, Hannah stopped bustling around the kitchen and paused to study her companion's expression. "Why on earth not?''

Rachel had long ago made up her mind that such a personal query deserved no answer. This time, however, she was too overwrought by all her conflicting emotions to listen to her own sensible warnings. Of all the people in her life, Hannah Brody was probably the best choice as a confidante—and the one most likely to keep her secret.

Making a final decision, Rachel looked around to be certain they were still alone, took a deep breath and blurted, "I can't have children, okay?"

Hannah's eyes widened. "What? You sure?"

"Positive. Well, almost," Rachel said. "I've been to three specialists and they all told me the same thing." Sighing, she added, "Please keep this to yourself. I've accepted the idea but I know my mother won't."

"Why not? You come by your problems naturally, Rachel. Martha was the same way. She'll probably be hoppin' mad at me for tellin' you, but it's time somebody did."

"Is that why you gave me that hush-up look in church? Did Mom try to have more children besides me?"

"Never quit. Not till your daddy passed on. After that, I guess she started thinkin' more like a grandma. She's always loved children, probably as much as you do."

"Then, why didn't they adopt a brother or sister for me?"

"You know why. Folks around here set a lot of store by kinship, by blood ties. Always have. Likely as not they always will. That's why I'm glad Sam's relatives are comin' for her, after all. I'll be sorry to see her go, but it'll be for the best. Family should stick together.''

Though she disagreed, at least in Samantha's case, Rachel kept her opinions to herself. She understood the mind-set that had led to Hannah's conclusion. Everyone she knew had grown up believing that blood relationships were more important than anything else. That kind of thinking was part of their culture. In fairness to Craig, he wasn't acting any differently than most men would—than her own father and mother apparently had.

Which was all the more reason for her to remain single, Rachel reasoned. Clearly, Martha wanted a grandchild by birth, just as she'd wanted only a child who was born into the family—which did answer one nagging question.

"Then, there's no chance I'm adopted?" Rachel asked.

Hannah cackled. "Silly goose. 'Course not. Your mama would never of agreed to somethin' like that.''

The back door banged. Rachel's head snapped around. Sean! She'd gotten so caught up in the emotional discussion she'd temporarily forgotten he was nearby! She was thankful there was nothing in his expression to imply he'd overheard what she'd just told Hannah. Matter of fact, he wasn't even looking at either of them. Instead, he was focused on the pretty little girl he carried.

Samantha had one arm around Sean's neck. In her

other hand was an empty basket for gathering eggs. Giggling and talking a mile a minute, she was monopolizing him as only an enthusiastic child can. Sean was grinning, nodding and giving the little girl his rapt attention.

Rachel smiled. Seeing two people she loved, together like that, was such a beautiful, dear sight that it brought tears to her eyes. What a wonderful father Sean would make some day!

For an unguarded moment Rachel let herself imagine being the third party in the make-believe family portrait. More tears gathered, wetting her lashes and threatening to spill over. She had to admit the futility of a dream like that.

Not wanting anyone to notice how unhappy she was, she quickly looked away.

The last thing she glimpsed before she turned her head was an unspoken question in Sean's eyes.

With Hannah controlling most of the adult conversation during the impromptu meal, and Samantha so excited to have both her teacher and counselor there that she babbled incessantly, Rachel didn't have to participate often. When she did choose to speak, she kept it short and to the point. She didn't see how she could get into much trouble with ''Please pass the gravy,'' although the way her life had been stirred up lately, there was no telling.

To her consternation, Sean seemed to be taking the

whole encounter quite calmly, even when Hannah began to quiz him about his background. And, to the Brodys' credit, they didn't react negatively to his announcement that, yes, he was a Yankee. Amused, Rachel came to the conclusion that true Southern hospitality knew no bounds. *Well, almost none.*

Allowing herself a moment to appreciate her roots, she dropped her guard, smiled and glanced over at Sean. He was looking straight at her! Instantly he broke into a wide grin, eyes sparkling. Rachel wanted to avert her gaze but she was mesmerized by the sight of his apparent bliss.

He leaned back and sighed with contentment. ''I believe that's the best meal I've ever eaten,'' he said. ''I couldn't hold another bite if you paid me.''

''Not even a piece of homemade apple pie?'' Hannah was beaming with pride.

''Homemade?''

''Made it myself just this mornin'.''

Rachel had to laugh at the funny, distressed look on Sean's face. ''Hannah's famous for her pies. If you're really too full to eat it now, maybe she'll let you take a piece home with you.''

''That would be great!'' He looked to his hostess. ''Ma'am?''

The older woman acted as if she didn't care, but Rachel could tell how pleased she was to have been asked. ''Oh, I 'spose. No sense lettin' it go to waste. I'm fixin' to bake cookies tomorrow, anyway.'' She smiled down at Samantha. The child had crawled up in Sean's lap as soon as he'd pushed away from the table. "Gotta get 'em done afore my little friend leaves."

Rachel stiffened. "Leaves?"

Hannah looked ashamed. "Sorry. I shouldn't of talked out of turn. Not when we're all havin' so much fun." She stared pointedly at the child, then turned to Rachel with a warning shake of her head. "Nothing's definite."

That was a lie if Rachel had ever heard one. She knew Hannah well enough to see right through her, especially since the older woman's eyes had grown suddenly misty when she'd mentioned Samantha's imminent departure.

Needing moral support, Rachel looked to Sean. He, too, was showing concern over the unexpected disclosure. He leaned down to whisper something in Samantha's ear, then set her on her feet and stood as if preparing to leave.

Rachel didn't want him to get away until she'd had a chance to speak privately with him, yet she also wanted the opportunity to find out exactly what Hannah was holding back. She took the initiative.

Starting to stack plates she said, "We'll help you clean up these dishes, won't we, Sean?"

To her delight he pitched right in and grabbed the bowls that had held potatoes and brown gravy. Rachel pointed to the meat platter. "Shall I put the roast away on this plate or do you want to put it on something smaller?''

"You two young folks just leave that table be," Hannah ordered, fists on her ample hips. "You're my guests. We'll see to the dishes. Hank always helps me soon as he gets the stock fed, anyways." She smiled fondly. "Sam, why don't you take your teacher and her friend outside and show 'em the chickens? I've been lettin' one old broody hen run loose and I figure she's made her a nest. See if y'all can find that, too. But leave it be if you do. I'd like her to raise a batch."

That notion made Rachel frown. "Isn't it pretty late in the year to be starting baby chicks?"

"Nope," Hannah said, shaking her head in silent warning.

Rachel understood. "Okay. We'll be right outside if you need us. But before I go home, you and I are going to have a serious talk."

"'Fraid so. Now, scat, the three of you."

Leading the way and talking nonstop, Samantha let the screen door bang behind her and skipped on ahead to start her search.

Sean held the door for Rachel, then followed her out onto the back porch. Pausing, he took a slow, deep breath and released it as a sigh.

"I'm beginning to think I may have made a mistake when I chose this career."

"Why?"

"Because I don't seem to be able to stay objective."

"About Samantha, you mean? I know. I'm having the same trouble. When Hannah slipped up and told us she was leaving pretty soon, I felt awful."

Sean reached for Rachel's hand, grasped it gently, then said, "We have only a very short time."

"What?" She clasped his fingers tighter. "How do you know?"

"Hank told me. I caught him out here before dinner and he filled me in. I mean before *supper.*"

"Dinner, supper—who cares?" Rachel stared up at him, her eyes pleading. "Exactly how much time did he say we had left?"

"Less than a week."

"Oh, no. Oh, Sean…"

Suddenly, it no longer mattered that she'd vowed to keep her distance from him. There was solace in his embrace and she needed that moral support a lot more than she needed to maintain her stupid pride.

Releasing his hand Rachel stepped into his arms, knowing he'd accept her and hoping he'd understand that her motives were innocent.

Sean pulled her close and laid his cheek against her silky hair, breathing in the sweetness of it and allowing himself to relish the tender moment. Like it or not, they shared a love for a special little girl and were about to experience a mutual loss when she was sent away.

Under those circumstances, leaning on each other, literally and figuratively, couldn't be wrong. Ill-advised maybe, but certainly not wrong. Saying good-bye to Samantha—for good—was going to be rough on everyone involved.

That realization had already settled in his heart and made it ache. How much more was it going to hurt when Samantha left them. And if he was so miserable, it must be a lot worse for a loving, maternal person like Rachel.

Filled with empathy, he turned his head a fraction and kissed her hair, finding the spot damp from his own silent tears.

Chapter Fourteen

Samantha's excited shout brought Rachel and Sean to their senses. By the time the child dashed around the corner to rejoin them, they were standing apart and trying to appear unaffected.

"I found it!" Samantha grabbed Rachel's hand and dragged her away. "Come see! Come see!"

Still fighting to maintain what little was left of her dignity, Rachel glanced back to tell Sean, "You'd better come, too, in case she's right. Broody hens can be pretty testy if they're disturbed."

Several long strides brought him even with the woman and child. "Think you'll need protection?"

Rachel looked up at him. "Tall. We need tall and you're it. If a hen starts to kick up a fuss, anybody close to the ground is going to get scratched. Including me."

Sean chuckled. "Are you saying you want me to pick you up?"

"No! Of course not. Just grab Samantha and keep her out of harm's way."

"Okay." In one fluid motion he scooped the little girl into his arms and held her while she protested, "Let me go! I wanna show you."

"You can show us from up there," Rachel said calmly. "Mama chickens can be really mean. Tell me where you think you saw the nest, and I'll check it out for you."

Samantha pouted. "No fair. I found it first."

"And we'll let you look again, just as soon as I've made sure it's safe. I know Mrs. Brody wouldn't have sent us to look for a nest if she'd thought we'd actually find one."

"There," the child said, pointing. "Under that big bush."

"This one?" Cautious, Rachel pushed back the lower branches of a thick crepe myrtle and peered through the greenery to the ground. The straw Hannah had used for mulch was slightly concave in one small spot but there were no eggs in sight. The depression certainly didn't resemble any nests Rachel had seen chickens scratch out before.

She relaxed. "You can put her down," she told Sean. "There's nothing under here."

"Yes, there is!" Samantha hit the ground running and dived under the shrubbery before either adult could stop her. Her shrill voice cried, "See? Right here. Oh," then went very still.

Rachel crouched. Sean dropped to his hands and knees and edged forward. They both heard Samantha cooing.

"Look," the child whispered. She turned, cradling something tiny and brown against her chest. "It's so soft."

"Aww, that's a baby bunny," Rachel gently told her. "You should put it back so its mother can take care of it."

"Maybe it doesn't have a mother," Samantha argued.

"Of course it has a mother. Everything does."

"Uh-uh. Maybe she got killed. Like my mama."

Overcome with guilt for having spoken so carelessly, Rachel didn't dare say anything else right away. Not without the catch in her throat making her voice break. She was grateful when Sean filled the gap.

"Tell you what," he said. "Let's put the baby back in its nest and I'll help you check on it every day after school. If it looks like its mother is really missing, then we'll give it something to eat. Okay?"

"There's two of them," Samantha said. "Twins."

"All the more reason to put it back. You wouldn't want its brother to be lonesome, would you?"

"It's a sister," Samantha announced. "They're girls. I know 'cause they're both so pretty and soft."

Smiling, Sean cast Rachel a sidelong glance. "I'm glad we cleared that up."

"Me, too." Rachel couldn't help but return his grin. "I knew better than to ask."

She held a group of branches back so the little girl could reach the hidden nest more easily. Samantha tucked the bunny next to its sibling beneath the loose straw and reemerged looking forlorn.

"You did the right thing," Rachel told her. "It's the job of people to take good care of all the animals."

"Like Noah did?" Samantha asked.

"Yes. Kind of."

Already eagerly following another train of thought, the child said, "Noah had lions and tigers and stuff. I saw pictures in Sunday school. I did. And giraffes, too. They stuck their head out the windows of the boat."

Rather than try to explain the immense scope of the actual ark the way the Bible did, Rachel merely said, "That's right. He had two of everything."

"I never saw a real giraffe," Samantha said, "or lions and stuff, either. My daddy was going to take me but…"

"I'm so sorry." Pulling her close, Rachel gave her a long hug before she let go and straightened. "I'm sure you'll get to go to the zoo someday, honey."

Eyes twinkling, Samantha grabbed her hand. "I know! *You* could take me. You and Sean!"

Rachel's gaze darted to his face and found her own surprise mirrored there. "I don't think so."

Sean shrugged, smiled. "Why not? You're a teacher. You're allowed to take kids on field trips, aren't you?"

"Yes, but it can take weeks to get a trip authorized."

"Okay. Then, we'll go privately."

"Hannah can't permit that," Rachel argued.

"How about if she goes along, too?"

"Are you saying we should take her with us?"

He wasn't about to back down. "Sure. Why not?"

"If we're going to do that, why not just give Hannah some money and send her while we're both at work?"

"And miss all the fun? Not me," Sean vowed. "I haven't been to a zoo in I don't know how long."

"Well, I'm not about to play hooky from school, if that's what you have in mind," Rachel said flatly.

"Don't our contracts say we get personal leave days or something like that?"

"Yes, but…"

"No more excuses, then. It's settled. We're going to the zoo. All of us." At his feet, the excited little girl was jumping up and down and squealing with delight.

Rachel wasn't quite as thrilled. She stared up at him. "Okay, smarty. When?"

"Soon."

"Not if we can't officially get the time off. I'd never ditch school. What kind of example would that be for my class?"

"A lousy one," Sean said with a sigh. "The question is, how badly do you want to keep from disappointing poor Sam."

Glancing around the immediate area, Rachel said, "Speaking of which, where did she go?"

"Probably ran inside to tell Hannah the good news."

"Terrific."

Shaking her head incredulously and staring off into the distance, Rachel wondered absently how she'd been coerced into agreeing to participate in such a crazy scheme. It didn't take her long to admit the truth—she wanted to go with Samantha and Sean so badly she could taste it.

So much for maintaining emotional distance from her students! She grimaced as her thoughts spiraled further. *Students?* Ha! They were nowhere near the worst of her problems. No, sir. Her biggest dilemma stood six feet tall and had enticingly mischievous eyes, not to mention an inherent kindness and the sort of physique that lonely women's dreams were made of.

Sean tapped her on the shoulder to regain her attention. "Hey there. Anybody home?"

"Nobody sane," Rachel quipped. "If I were, I'd

have told you I wasn't going anywhere with you, let alone to the zoo.''

"But you didn't," he countered, grinning. "And you know how important it is to keep a promise to an impressionable child. Shall we plan on the day after tomorrow?"

"Will that be soon enough?"

"Barely," Sean said, sobering. "Just barely."

By the day of the trip Rachel was convinced that the Lord must have had His hand in their outing. Otherwise, how could all their plans have panned out so beautifully? Standing in Hannah's yard, waiting for Sean to arrive, she said as much.

"Know what ya mean," the older woman agreed. "When I told Mr. Vanbruger that Sam would be leaving soon, he said she could keep up with her schoolwork at home till then. 'Course, it ain't like you give her much homework in kindergarten."

Rachel laughed lightly. "True. But we learn new things every day. What I can't believe is how easily he approved my request for time off, even though the year's just beginning. I hope he was as generous with Sean."

"You didn't ask him?"

"I haven't seen him. Not to talk to. The closest I've come to that man since we ran into each other over here the other night was a few glimpses of him in the hallways at school. He didn't bother to telephone me, either. If it hadn't been for you, I wouldn't even have known what time we were supposed to be leaving or where we were going to meet.''

All Hannah said was "Hmm," before she turned away and went back into the house, leaving Rachel free to concentrate more fully on her innermost thoughts.

The thing that surprised her was her own level of enthusiasm for the trip. From the moment she'd awakened that morning she'd felt like a child herself. At first she'd assumed she was merely happy on Samantha's behalf, but now that she'd had time to look deeper into her heart she had to admit that much of her joy was personal.

Such a sudden awakening brought Rachel up short. It wasn't right to let herself make believe that her life could turn out differently than she knew it would. Yet she desperately wanted one day—just one day—when she could pretend there was hope, that she might someday become someone's mother. Someone's wife.

Her breath caught. She stood very still, listening to her racing heart and acknowledging the whole truth. She didn't dream of being just anyone's wife—she dreamed of belonging only to Sean Bates, and he to her.

"But I love him, Father," she whispered. "I can't do that to him. I can't deny him a family. What am I going to do?"

For a moment she considered asking God to change

her body so she could feel complete. It wouldn't have been the first time she'd begged for healing. When Craig had taken the news of her physical lack so hard, she'd fallen on her knees as soon as she was alone and wept an unspoken plea. At that time, the Lord had granted her peace instead. To continue to ask Him for something else seemed ungrateful. Wrong-hearted.

Before Rachel could pursue that conviction further she heard a car approaching. The screen door banged behind her. She intercepted Samantha flying down the porch steps and used the child's momentum to swing her around twice before cautiously releasing her with a gentle warning.

"Slow down, sweetie. Let the poor man park before you mob him, okay? You know it's not safe to run out in the road when a car's coming."

Samantha acted as if she didn't hear a word. As soon as Rachel let go of her, she barreled up to Sean's car and tugged on the handle of the driver's door.

Grinning, he opened it and gave her a hug. "Hi, there, kiddo. You ready to go?"

"Yeah!"

He looked past the wiggling child to the woman standing at the base of the stairs. "Looks like you are, too. Very nice."

Nervous, Rachel smoothed the hem of her knit shirt over the waistband of her shorts and smiled. "Thanks. I know we'll have a lot of walking to do and it's bound to be hot today. I wanted to be comfortable."

"Hey, don't apologize to me," Sean said. "I think you look great."

Modesty made her counter, "With these short legs?"

"They reach the ground, so they must be long enough," he teased. "Is Hannah ready to go?"

Rachel nodded. "She just ducked back into the house a minute ago. Stay there. I'll go get her."

Watching the petite woman whirl and dash up the porch steps, Sean was taken with her youthful exuberance and upbeat attitude. Such qualities were definitely a gift, he reasoned, although he wasn't quite ready to credit the Almighty as the giver.

He did have to admit there was something odd about living among so many believers, though. Most days, not an hour went by that someone didn't mention a Higher Power. Christianity was such an integral part of everyone's life here, it seemed that even those who didn't profess a particular denominational faith knew the Bible and gave credit to God for even the smallest blessing. Speaking of which...

Sean heard Samantha babbling about the baby rabbits she'd found and saw her gesturing wildly toward the nest. "What?"

"They're gone," she told him. "I looked and looked. Maybe they got lost."

"Or got big enough to leave home. Maybe it was time for them to go to kindergarten, like you."

Hands on her hips, the child made a silly face. "Bunnies don't go to school!"

"Are you sure?" Sean couldn't help laughing at the way she was posturing. It reminded him of the way Rachel acted whenever she was miffed.

"Positive."

"Okay. If you say so." He glanced up with an expectant grin as the front door opened again. "Here comes Miss Rachel and Mrs. Brody. Time to go. Get in the back seat, and I'll fasten your safety belt."

"I want Miss Rachel to ride with me!"

"That's what I was afraid of," Sean murmured. "Okay. This is your trip. We'll do it your way."

By the time he'd secured Samantha's belt, however, only Rachel had come as far as the car. She was frowning. Sean looked from her to Hannah and back. "What's the matter?"

"Hannah says her blood sugar is too high again. She doesn't feel well enough to go with us."

"Oh-oh."

Rachel nodded sagely. "Oh-oh is right. *Now* what are we going to do?"

"Well, I don't know about you, but I'm going to the zoo."

"We shouldn't."

"Mrs. Brody doesn't seem to mind. See? She's waving."

"I know. I suggested we take Hank, instead, so

we'd have an authorized foster parent along. She just laughed at me.''

''No wonder. Can you imagine old Hank at the zoo? He'd probably spend all his time telling the keepers they weren't taking care of the animals properly.''

Rachel smiled at his accurate assessment. ''Probably.'' She leaned down to look at the child already ensconced in the back seat of Sean's car, then sighed noisily as she conceded. ''Okay. I'll go. But if I get in trouble over this I'm going to blame the whole thing on you.''

''Fair enough. Want me to tie you up, sling you over my shoulder like a pirate and throw you in the car to make your story more convincing?''

He burst out laughing when she gave him the Samantha Smith pose of indignation and said, ''No, thanks. I'll pass.''

There were two large zoos within a reasonable driving distance of Serenity—one in Little Rock and one in Memphis. Both were a three-hour journey. Sean decided to go to Memphis because he also wanted to give Samantha the opportunity to see the Mississippi River. Long before they reached the Tennessee/Arkansas border, however, she'd fallen fast asleep in the back seat.

''I'm glad you rode up front with me,'' he told

Rachel. "Our little friend has conked out. Guess I'll have to show her the Big Muddy on our way home."

"I had to sit where I could see out," Rachel replied. "The road between Hardy and Blackrock is way too crooked. It always makes me dizzy."

"Sorry. Do you get seasick, too?"

She shrugged, taking care to keep her eyes on the road in case there was a curve ahead. "I don't know. The only boat I was ever in was a canoe. A friend and I floated down the Strawberry River. We went so slowly I hardly noticed movement."

"Someday we'll have to take a trip in a real boat, then."

When she didn't comment, Sean glanced over at her. Her hands were clasped tightly together in her lap. Her jaw was clamped shut. Her beautiful blue eyes were staring out the windshield, concentrating as if she were the one driving.

Wisely, he dropped the subject. It had been stupid to talk to Rachel about the future. She was right. There was no use prolonging the agony by pretending they had a chance as a couple. Thanks to his big mouth, she already knew he came from a dysfunctional family—one she'd not want to even consider joining. Nor would she want to bring into the world children who might exhibit that same propensity for addiction.

Geneticists were still split on whether or not such leanings were inherited, but Sean wasn't about to chance finding out they were. So far, he'd escaped the insidious addiction that had swallowed up his father and brothers, yet they all came from the same ancestors. If he ever let himself slip, no telling how far down he'd slide before he hit bottom.

His hands tightened on the wheel, his knuckles whitening from the effort. No way was he going to involve an innocent woman like Rachel in such a terrible life. She deserved better. Much better than he could ever offer.

To distract himself before his musings made him too depressed, he handed her a Tennessee road map. "Here. I checked before we left, and I think if we get off on Poplar we can take it all the way to the zoo. See if that's right, will you? The off-ramp should be coming up pretty soon."

"Okay. As long as you don't go around any corners while I'm not watching the road."

"If any come along I'll straighten them just for you," he quipped, quickly adding, "Oops! Hang on. Corner coming up."

She blinked and focused on the roadway as best she could. It was several long seconds before her equilibrium returned to normal. "Whew! That was fun. Remind me not to eat anything for a couple of hours before we start home."

"*Eat?* What if the zoo doesn't sell rabbit food?"

"Very funny. I don't eat salads all the time. I happen to love hot dogs. Ice cream, too, although I don't usually indulge when I have my whole class along on a field trip.''

''Why not?''

''Because it's not fair to give myself a treat when my students can't have the same thing. It's way too messy. Bus drivers really hate it when you bring twenty-five or thirty sticky kids back on board for the ride home.''

''Speaking from experience, I have to agree.'' Sean nodded toward the back seat. ''Tell you what. If you and Sleeping Beauty promise to wash afterwards, you can both have all the ice cream you want.''

Rachel raised an eyebrow. ''I'm so relieved to have your permission, Mr. Bates. Thanks bunches.''

''You don't have to get sarcastic. I was just trying to make polite conversation.''

''I know. Sorry. When you mentioned driving the bus it made me think about school again. Neither of us may have jobs if the authorities find out Hannah didn't come with us. I guess worrying about that has made me a little cranky.''

''You? Why should you worry? Everybody I meet keeps telling me God will take care of them. Don't you believe the same thing?''

She gave a derisive huff. ''It's not that simple. If I suspect that what I'm doing may be wrong, then for me it *is* wrong. I can't count on divine providence to step in and rescue me if my own folly has gotten me into trouble.''

"What we're doing here can't be wrong," he insisted. "This is our last chance to show Sam a good time, to let her know we care about her. No matter where she goes or what happens in the future, she'll always have today to remember."

So will I, Rachel mused. *So will I.*

Remembering was going to be easy. It was forgetting that was going to be hard.

A child and a zoo are more than compatible, they're symbiotic, Rachel thought, watching Samantha run from one exhibit to the next with Sean in tow. It had only taken the bright child a few attempts to figure out that she could get a much better view of everything if she asked Sean to hold her up instead of begging Rachel for a boost.

The only time that additional height wasn't helpful was in the tropical, walk-in aviary, where all the brightly hued birds flew freely overhead, as if still at home in the jungle. The rest of the zoo followed a stylized Egyptian theme, in keeping with the Memphis name, and featured gardens brimming with flowers between each exhibit. No matter how many times Rachel visited there, its beauty always enthralled her.

Sean led the way to the elephant enclosure. Samantha was balanced on his shoulders, pointing and babbling. "She only loves me for my height," he said aside to Rachel.

"Speaking as someone who's been hanging out

pretty close to the ground her whole life, I can understand that fascination,'' she replied, smiling. ''I dare you to leave her up there while we eat the ice cream you promised us.''

''Only if you pick a flavor that doesn't clash with the color of my hair.''

Rachel laughed. She'd smiled and giggled so often since they'd been together that the muscles in her cheeks actually hurt. What a day this had been! What a marvelous, blessed day. If she were running the universe, the sun would never set. This very same day would go on forever and ever. And so would her happiness.

Their *shared* happiness, she corrected. From the outset, Samantha had acted as if being with the two of them was as routine as being with her former parents. And Sean played the part of father-shepherd with a natural grace and quiet wisdom.

Though Rachel had done her best to fit in, there were still unguarded moments when she felt like an outsider, a pretender, and had to hide behind her sunglasses to blink back tears.

If Sean noticed, he kept the observation to himself. Rachel was glad he hadn't quizzed her about it. Under the circumstances she had no intention of baring her soul. Especially not to him. Clearly, Samantha was delighted with the zoo trip, and Rachel didn't intend to do or say one single thing that might spoil it.

She smiled to herself, accepting the inevitable with

a dollop of cynicism. Yes, she'd miss Samantha. Terribly. And she'd always think of this outing with Sean as a high point of her life. But the tears weren't all for them. Not even close. Rachel's tears were for herself, for the one thing she wanted that she could never have—love and commitment.

Truth to tell, her mother had been right all along. A job wasn't enough. Being with Sean and Samantha all day had convinced her of that.

Like it or not, she did want a family of her own.

Desperately.

Chapter Fifteen

The drive back to Serenity seemed to take hours longer than the drive the other way. Rachel yawned. "Sorry. It's been a long day."

"Hang in there. We're almost to the Brodys'."

"I know." She smiled wistfully as she glanced at the dozing little girl in the back seat. "You shouldn't have bought her that enormous stuffed animal. It was way too expensive."

"Had to. This was my last chance to spoil her."

Rachel sighed. "I'm really going to miss her."

"Me, too."

Glancing sidelong at Sean she was certain she saw a glint of moisture in his eyes. "Do you think they'll let her write to us, or maybe phone if we tell them to reverse the charges?"

"Maybe," he said. "I suppose it all depends on

whether they're taking her because they really want her or because of her inheritance. Wait till they learn it's been placed into a trust fund so it can't be squandered.''

"Hannah did mention something about money coming to Samantha. How did you find out so much?''

"I asked. I'm surprised you didn't.''

"I suppose I should have. I just kept telling myself I couldn't do anything to change what would eventually happen, so I ought to stay out of it. Stupid, huh?''

"Avoiding heartache? No, that's not stupid. It's normal. Nobody goes out looking for dragons to slay unless they find monstrous footprints in their own backyard.''

Rachel's brow knit. "Huh?''

"Some people are born crusaders,'' Sean explained. "Others aren't. Your talent happens to be teaching and you do that well. You said you recognized the gift when you were very young.''

"Yes, I did.'' She was surprised he remembered a casual comment from so early in their relationship.

"Then, don't beat yourself up about not being gung-ho to do something else. You have character, Rachel. If you saw an injustice that needed righting, I know you'd try to right it. When there's nothing that can be done, staying out of the affairs of others is the smartest choice.''

"But I haven't. Not really," she said softly, in confidence, with a quick peek at the back seat to make sure Samantha was still asleep. "I was involved up to my eyebrows the minute I set eyes on that little girl."

All Sean said was "I know exactly what you mean."

The sun was set by the time they pulled into the driveway of the Brody house and parked. Apparently no one had thought to turn on the outside lights, leaving the yard dark except for the glow from the living room windows and a waxing moon that was starting to rise above the treetops.

Dimness suited Sean just fine. It matched his sinking mood. Leaving his hands resting on the steering wheel, he sighed and looked over at Rachel. "Well, I suppose we'd better wake her up and get this over with."

"I suppose so." She managed a smile. "I want to thank you for talking me into going along. I had a wonderful time. I'm sure Sam did, too."

"Hey!" Sean said, brightening. "You called her Sam. That's a real breakthrough."

"Better late than never, I guess."

Slowly, deliberately, Rachel turned in her seat and got to her knees so she could lean over the back of the front seat and gently rouse the weary child. She touched Samantha's shoe, wiggled it. "Honey? Wake up. We're home."

Samantha snuggled closer to her stuffed panda and rubbed her cheek on its soft fur. Still asleep she murmured, "Mama."

Tears sprang to Rachel's eyes. Hiding her ragged emotions she quickly got out of the car and stood with her back to it, arms folded across her chest. When Sean came up behind her, laid his arms over hers and pulled her close, his tenderness cost her the last vestiges of her self-control and she began to weep.

"I...I'm sorry," she said. "I wasn't going to do this."

"It's okay. I have broad shoulders."

"No kidding."

As he slowly leaned down and kissed the top of her head, she dashed away her tears, turned and said the first thing that popped into her mind. "You missed."

"I what?"

"You missed." Through her misty gaze she saw understanding dawn as she pointed to her trembling lips. "It goes there."

"Does it?" Sean whispered. "Are you sure?"

"No. But do it, anyway."

He bent his head, more than ready to give her the kiss she was asking for. He'd been longing to end their marvelous day together in exactly that loving way. Only the belief that Rachel wouldn't welcome the romantic overture had stopped him. Now that she'd removed that obstacle, he was overjoyed to oblige.

Rachel rose on tiptoe, waiting, anticipating, re-membering. She could feel Sean's breath, warm on her face, see the flicker of desire lighting his eyes. One more chapter in the fairy tale, she promised her-self. Just one more and then it would be all over. For good.

Her lips parted. Her hands slipped around his neck. The moment she sensed his strong arms around her, she trusted him completely, and felt him raise her enough to lift her feet off the ground. Lost in that precious moment, Rachel started to close her eyes.

Bright light suddenly blinded her. Sean started and almost dropped her.

She staggered, fighting for balance and calling upon her heightened perceptions to make sense of whatever had just occurred. Floodlights illuminated the front yard, trapping them in the shadow thrown by his car. Rachel was instantly glad they'd been standing on the side opposite the house instead of sharing their kiss on the porch where they'd be easily seen.

Shouting and cursing was coming from the direc-tion of the house. It built to a cacophony of deeply disturbing sound. The front door slammed, then slammed again.

Still blinking against the brightness, Rachel shaded

her eyes with one hand. When she reached out to touch Sean's arm with the other she felt his muscles flex beneath her fingers. "What's going on?"

"I don't know." He tried to maneuver her behind him. "Stay back till we find out."

She resisted. "Don't be silly. Hannah wouldn't let anything bad happen to us here. Neither would Hank. He may be old but he's strong as a bull."

Peering up at the porch she counted five adults. Hannah and Hank were there, of course, arm in arm. The only other person Rachel recognized was—oh, no! It looked like Heatherington! Now the fat was in the fire for sure!

A middle-aged couple Rachel had never seen before broke away from the others and started down the porch steps toward the car. The smartly dressed woman left her portly mate lagging behind, stomped straight up to Sean and wagged a long finger in his face.

"How dare you! Do you know how late it is? We've all been worried sick. Field trip, my eye. I'll see you're *fired*. Both of you."

Sean kept his voice low. "We're very sorry you were inconvenienced, Mrs...." He tried Samantha's last name. "Smith, is it?"

"You know very well it is," she screeched. "No alibis. You tried to steal my niece and you're not going to get away with it. Not if I have any say in the matter."

Rachel stepped forward, still squinting and shading her eyes. "That's not what happened at all. We just wanted to show her a good time before she left us."

"Don't give me that. Ms. Heatherington told these people we were coming all the way down here to pick her up, and you didn't even have the courtesy to have her here." The woman muttered a curse. "Good thing you came back when you did. I was about to call the cops. Maybe I still will."

"That won't be necessary," Sean said calmly. "Apparently there was some mix-up about the exact time of your arrival." He gestured at his car. "As you can see, Samantha's fine. She's right here. Safe and sound."

"Then, give her to me. I don't intend to stand around all night and argue."

Rachel opened the car door and leaned inside.

Standing close by, Sean heard her mumble, "You could have fooled me," before her tone changed to gently rouse Samantha. "Come on, honey. Wake up. We're home. And there are some new people here I want you to meet."

Sean was proud of the way she put aside her own needs to do what was best for the child. If it was tearing him up to think of handing Samantha over to the rigid, unforgiving person they'd just encountered, what must poor Rachel be thinking? One quick look at her face told him exactly what she was going through, and it made his heart ache for her.

Clinging to her beloved teacher the child rubbed sleep out of her eyes while Rachel stroked her thin back and urged her more awake. She looked as if she was about to hand Samantha to her new guardian when the woman reached out, grabbed the little girl's wrist and wrenched her away!

Rachel screamed, ''No!''

Sean put his arm around her in consolation and restraint.

Hannah Brody had been hanging back, watching. Now, she bustled up and started to call the other woman every nasty name Rachel had ever heard—and a few she hadn't—while Samantha wailed at their feet and the social worker dithered in the background.

The Smith woman paused only long enough to tell the child to shut up, then said, ''Come on, Robert. Bring her,'' and stormed off.

''Yes, Daphne.'' With a shrug, the man held out his hand. Instead of taking it, Samantha clung to Rachel.

The little girl's weeping had intensified almost to the point of hysteria, and Sean was worried about her mental state. He had begun considering intercession the moment he'd encountered Samantha's new guardians. Now that Daphne Smith had demonstrated such a horrific lack of compassion and tact, he was beginning to think they might actually stand a chance of heading off the change of custody. It was worth a try. Staying with the Brodys indefinitely would be far better for Sam than going to live with the part of her extended family he'd just met.

Rachel was on her knees trying to soothe the weeping child when more shouting began. Hank and Robert were getting into it now. Younger and heavier, Robert threw a punch at Hank. He missed. Hank fell, anyway, when he staggered backward to escape the blow. Yelling, Hannah launched herself, fists flailing, into the midst of the melee.

Sean wasn't far behind. He pulled Hannah out of the fracas, but she dove back in before he had a chance to rescue Hank.

Clearly, someone should telephone the police, Rachel decided—but who? Hank, Hannah, Sean and the Smiths were all part of the problem. And it didn't look like Ms. Heatherington was in any shape to help, either. The usually staid social worker stood frozen in place, her mouth agape, staring at the near riot from the relative safety of the porch.

It was evidently up to Rachel to make the call if anyone was going to. What the whole group needed was a cooling-off period, and she knew she wasn't big enough or tough enough to send them to separate corners the way she did her kindergarten students when they misbehaved.

Preparing to go inside to use the Brody's phone, she straightened and reached for Samantha's hand so she could keep her close. The child must have misunderstood. Instead of meekly taking her teacher's offered hand, she jerked away and dashed down the dirt driveway.

Rachel was caught off guard. "Samantha! Wait!"

The little girl didn't pay any heed. Already in a frenzy, she increased her speed. The last good glimpse Rachel got of her before the night swallowed her up was the bobbing of her blond curls and the dusky white of her tennis shoes.

"Sean!" Rachel hollered at the top of her lungs, then took off in pursuit without waiting to see if he'd heard.

The driveway was dark and winding. There were no streetlights along Squirrel Hill Road, either, so the farther Rachel got from the Brody house the more the countryside blended into a murky blur, lit only by a sliver of the moon.

"Samantha!" she shouted. "Wait! Please."

Behind her she heard Sean's voice echoing her calls. Just knowing he was following gave Rachel confidence. Her legs were already tired from a whole day of walking. The muscles throbbed, threatening to fail. She tripped. Faltered. Recovered.

"Oh, please, Lord," she prayed aloud. "Help me!"

Arms held out in front of her, she groped along, hoping she wouldn't accidentally bump into one of Hank's barbed-wire fences and praying Samantha knew enough about the lay of the land to keep herself safe, even in the near dark.

By Rachel's reckoning there was only the cement crossing over the wet-weather creek left to negotiate before she reached the road. The smack of her rubber-soled shoes hitting the hard concrete of the swale confirmed that conclusion.

She stopped there, fighting to hold her breath long enough to listen for Samantha's footsteps up ahead. Instead, she heard the pounding of a runner's stride somewhere behind. Sean was coming! Thank God!

A quick breath later she heard another sound. The way noise echoed in the narrow, wooded valley it was hard to tell what direction it was coming from, or even what it was. She listened carefully. The roar was growing more definable. It had to be a car or a pickup truck. And it sounded like it was headed their way on Squirrel Hill Road!

Panic chilled Rachel to the depths of her soul. Even the most levelheaded five-year-old was liable to forget safety rules in a moment of excitement. Samantha was unlikely to remember anything, let alone an admonition to stay out of the street.

Rachel sprinted for the road, praying all the way. The car's motor was getting louder and louder.

She could see headlight beams now, brilliant and blinding. Between her position and that of the speeding car she caught a glimpse of a small, moving shadow.

It might be a deer, her subconscious insisted. And what if it wasn't? With no thought for personal safety,

Rachel ran out into the road, waving her arms wildly over her head and shouting, "Sam! Look out!"

Behind her, Sean gave a guttural roar when he saw her luminescent silhouette aglow in the glare of oncoming headlights.

The driver braked. Skidded. The car started to slide sideways, tires screeching.

Sean lunged for Rachel. Everything seemed to be moving in slow motion. Airborne for what seemed like ages, he finally got his arms around her. He twisted to use his own body to cushion her fall and they landed in a heap by the side of the road. The vehicle came to rest mere feet away in the same shallow ditch, its lights blurred by tall grasses and brush.

Irrationally angry, Sean bellowed at her, "Are you *crazy?* What did you think you were doing?"

Rachel was wobbly when he helped her to her feet. "Sam," she gasped. "Samantha. Did you see her?"

"No. Where?"

He scanned the darkness beyond the car. In the distance he could see small lights bobbing down the driveway from the Brody house. It looked as if several people were sensibly using flashlights to guide them.

"I don't know where," Rachel said. She sagged against him. "I thought I saw her just before…before the crash."

Refusing to let go when he knew he'd come so close to losing her moments before, he said, "Okay.

Show me what you think you saw. We'll look together. Then I'll come back and see about the driver."
He sneered in the direction of the car. "The guy's
probably feeling no pain. I can smell the booze from
here."

"Over that way." Rachel pointed with a shaky
hand.

Sean didn't like the tremulousness of her voice.
He'd never heard her sound so weak, so dispirited.
"Can you make it?"

"I'm fine," she lied. "Hurry."

"Looks like the cavalry's almost here," Sean told
her, indicating the Brody driveway. "Let's wait. We
can borrow their flashlights instead of stumbling
around in the dark."

Rachel wasn't willing to delay. She grabbed his
hand and forged ahead. "No. I'm sure I saw something. I…" Her legs suddenly gave way.

Sean caught her before she fell. He didn't have to
ask what was wrong. He could see for himself.

They'd found Samantha.

No one argued with Rachel when she was chosen
to accompany the unconscious child to the hospital.
Her own bumps and bruises from the near miss with
the out-of-control car were her ticket to ride in the
same ambulance. She'd have suffered the injuries
gladly to earn the opportunity to comfort the poor girl.

Unfortunately, Samantha remained unconscious.

Patting her cool, limp, little hand, Rachel kept asking the paramedics, "Why doesn't she come to?"

"We won't know till we get some tests run," one of them answered. "We're taking good care of her. Why don't you lie down until we get to the emergency room, ma'am?"

Rachel was adamant. "No. She needs me."

"There's nothing you can do for her right now. You'd better take care of yourself so you'll be able to look after her when she wakes up."

"I'm fine. Just cold," Rachel said, shivering.

"That's from shock." The medic gently wrapped a gray blanket around her shoulders, guided her to the spare gurney and lifted her feet to swing her whole body around.

The appeal of a moment's respite was so strong that she let him ease her down onto the pristine sheets and pillow. "Thanks."

"You're welcome," he said. "I understand how you feel. I've dealt with lots of mothers and they all act the same way when their kids get hurt."

Bone-weary and beyond responding, Rachel closed her eyes and turned her face to the wall to hide her silent tears.

Chapter Sixteen

Sean had lingered at the accident scene just long enough to make sure Rachel and Samantha were safely aboard the ambulance, then headed for his car.

What he wanted more than anything was to be reunited with Rachel. To comfort her as best he could. If things didn't turn out okay for little Sam he didn't know what either of them would do. He'd been so angry when that drunk driver was pulled out of the wrecked car and arrested he'd wanted to strangle the guy with his bare hands. It had taken several police officers—plus Hank Brody—to keep him from trying.

Right now, the ambulance bearing Sean's loved ones was headed for an emergency facility near Salem. He'd been told that if more specialized care was needed once initial assessments were made, one or both patients would be flown by helicopter to Little

Rock. He was determined to get to them before that. He had to. Nothing was more important.

His hands clamped the car's steering wheel, every muscle tense, as he raced on through the night. How totally helpless he felt! This was a situation where a strong belief in God, like Rachel had, would sure come in handy.

If there is a God, he countered.

But suppose there was? What would he say to Him?

Sean had no idea, nor did he think the Almighty would be inclined to listen to the prayers of a cynical guy like him. Why should He?

Maybe for Rachel's sake, Sean answered. For Rachel's sake he'd have to try.

Keeping his eyes on the road ahead he first drew a deep breath. "Hey, God? You up there?" he began. "It's me. No, forget that. I'm not asking for myself, I'm asking for Rachel. You know Rachel. She's one of Yours. She's probably too traumatized to ask for help herself right now so I'm asking in her place. And for Samantha, too. Okay?"

Sean felt silly talking to an invisible being. Next thing he knew he'd probably be seeing guardian angels the same way Samantha said she did.

Angels? A vivid recollection of the accident leapt into Sean's consciousness. He'd never forget the sight of Rachel bravely trying to flag down that oncoming car. Reflected light had played tricks with her appearance, making her waving arms look like wings in motion. That was how he'd known where she was. It was that glowing image he'd jumped for when he'd come running out of the Brody's driveway.

His heart started to pound erratically. That was *exactly* what had happened. No question about it. He was positive. So how had he and Rachel landed at least three car lengths up the road from the end of the drive, instead of beneath the wrecked car? If there was a logical, scientific explanation, he sure didn't know what it might be. Unless...

The urge to dismiss the notion of divine intervention was strong. Stronger still was his assurance that he'd been an unwitting part of something amazing.

His hands trembled on the steering wheel. His heart felt lodged in his throat. "God?" he whispered. "Jesus? Are You really out there?"

Though no audible answer came, Sean was certain there had been one. He was finding it hard to see the roadway through eyes misted by tears of intense gratitude. Cautiously he slowed his frenetic driving pace, while his heart threatened to pound its way out of his chest.

As the beginnings of faith touched him he sensed a subtle change in his outlook, a kind of peace he'd never felt before. It flowed over and through him like the passing of a warm wind or the rising of a blush to one's cheeks.

"Okay," he said, nodding resolutely. "You win,

God. If You want me, You've got me, although what You'd want with the likes of me, I sure can't imagine. Just keep taking care of the people I love, will You? Please? That's all I care about.''

Sean had barely finished speaking when he realized he'd arrived at the hospital. He cut the wheel hard to the right and drove straight to the emergency entrance. As he climbed out of his car it occurred to him that he'd just turned more than one hard corner to get to where he found himself right now.

Sean barged past the receptionist without asking anyone's permission and straight-armed the swinging door. The treatment room was crowded. He spotted Rachel pacing in front of a closed curtain. She had a blanket wrapped around her shoulders, her hair was a mess and her cheeks were pale and dirt-smeared, but she still looked wonderful to him.

He hurried across the room. ''Rachel!''

She didn't hesitate to step into his embrace. ''Oh, Sean.''

For a long moment he just held her, breathing in her familiar scent and giving silent thanks that she was okay. Finally he loosed his grip and looked at the curtain.

''Is Sam in there?''

''Yes.''

''How is she?''

''I don't know. They won't let me see her. The

doctors are with her right now. I've been trying to listen to what they're saying but it's too noisy in this big room.''

''At least they got to her right away. Have they checked you out yet?''

''No. I'll be fine as soon as I know Samantha's going to be all right. I've been going crazy, waiting and worrying.''

''I'm here now. We'll wait together.''

He turned, keeping one arm protectively around her shoulders. ''Come on. Let's sit down. You look awful.''

''Oh, thanks a heap.''

Sean gazed down at her tenderly. ''That's my girl. When you snap at me like that, I know you're okay.''

''I didn't snap at you for no reason,'' Rachel argued. ''You said I looked awful.''

''You've never looked better to me.'' There was a definite catch in his voice.

''Really?''

''Really.'' Once again realizing fully how close he'd come to watching her die, he couldn't convince himself to stop touching her, holding her close, so he sat down first and urged her onto his lap.

Rachel willingly settled there, wrapped in her warm blanket and the comforting arms of the man she loved. Tomorrow there would be plenty of time to explain why they ought to stop seeing each other.

Right now, all she wanted was to retreat from reality by cuddling up to Sean.

"I wish…" he began.

She raised her face to him. "What do you wish?"

"Nothing. You rest. Now's not the time to talk about it."

"Hmm. I wonder. After what happened tonight it seems to me that waiting too long to do *anything* can be a mistake."

"Maybe you're right this time."

"Maybe?" One eyebrow arched. "And what do you mean, *this time?*"

Rachel had intended her remarks to distract him and lift his spirits. She might be showing signs of stress, as he'd said, but so was he. If she looked half as world-weary as he did, it was no wonder he'd commented on it. To her relief, he smiled.

"Okay. Maybe you have been right more than once. And I have to admit I've been wrong—at least about a few things."

"Like what?"

"Kids, for one thing."

Rachel stiffened. "What kids?"

"Sam, to start with," Sean said. Rachel was just beginning to breathe again when he added, "and maybe having some of my own someday, too."

"That's nice."

"I thought you'd agree." He gave her a quick squeeze. "So, how about it?"

"How about what?"

"Kids? A family? You and me?"

She pushed herself away from him and struggled to her feet. "No, thanks."

The dejected expression on his face, in his eyes, hurt her to the core. The truth wouldn't wait. It wasn't fair to leave Sean wondering why she'd turned his proposal down flat. No matter how hard confession was going to be, he deserved to hear her reasons.

Drawing the blanket closer as a symbolic shield, Rachel stood at his feet and spoke softly. "I can't have children, Sean. You need to find a wife who can."

He stared up at her. So, *that* was it. No wonder she'd acted so upset when her mother had kept needling her about grandchildren. Martha must not know.

"Have you told anyone else?"

Rachel grimaced. "Only Hannah. And Craig. You know how that turned out—he dumped me."

Sean slowly got to his feet. There was a lopsided smile on his face that confused Rachel. He reached for her. She backed away, tripped on the dragging tail of the blanket and nearly fell. Sean righted her just as the curtain around Samantha's bed slid open.

They froze, staring at the emerging doctor. He was stripping off his gloves as he announced, "Your daughter's going to be fine."

Rachel was glad Sean's arms were around her shoulders again because her knees felt suddenly wobbly. She started to tell the doctor, "Samantha's not..." then felt the tightening of Sean's grip and realized there was a definite advantage to being considered the little girl's parents. There would be time enough to set the record straight after they'd spent some time at her bedside.

"She's not badly hurt?" Sean asked, filling in the gap in Rachel's response.

The doctor shook his head. "Doesn't appear to be. I'm going to go ahead and order a few tests, just to be sure. I really don't think you have anything to worry about."

"Thank God," Rachel breathed.

Beside her, Sean said, "I already did."

Samantha was wheeled to a private room as soon as the tests were completed. Rachel and Sean stood at her bedside, holding hands and watching her sleep.

"I can't believe she's going to get to stay in Arkansas," Rachel said. "What did Robert tell you while I was in being examined, anyway? Why the change of heart?"

"Apparently, Daphne didn't want the responsibility of a child in the first place. Being related, Robert felt guilty so he insisted on trying, but when he saw his wife with Sam he decided he'd made a big mistake and called everything off."

Rachel sighed. "Well, that's one worry behind us."

"Actually, it's *two*," Sean said quietly. He stepped closer to the woman he loved and gently caressed her shoulder. "You see, all along I've been bothered by the idea of having kids of my own. If you'd been listening closely, instead of worrying about your own problems, you might have figured that out."

"But…"

He laid a finger across her lips. "Hush. Let me finish. It took me a while to think it all through but I finally saw the light—in more ways than one. God knew what we both needed. He went out of His way to bring us together." Sean glanced briefly at the sleeping child. "He provided our first little girl, too."

Awed, Rachel could hardly believe her ears. She placed her hands flat on his chest and felt the rapid beating of his heart. Her own pulse wasn't exactly dawdling, either. "Do you think we'd have a chance," she breathed, "really?"

"Well, there is a catch. I'm afraid we'll have to get married."

"I could probably manage that," Rachel told him. "If you asked me properly."

A stirring from the bed prompted them to glance at Samantha. Though her eyes were still closed, Sean suspected she'd been listening. He leaned over her to whisper, "I'm about to ask Miss Rachel to marry me, kiddo, so pay close attention."

"Do you think she can hear us?" Rachel asked.

"Let's find out, shall we?" Sean dropped to one

knee. "Ms. Woodward, would you do me the honor of becoming my wife?"

"Yes!" She couldn't help giggling. "Now get up before the nurses think there's something wrong with you."

Sean immediately took her in his arms and swung her around, feet off the ground. "You said *yes!* What could possibly be wrong with me? I feel wonderful!"

From the direction of the bed came an answering giggle. Then a small voice asked, "Can we go home, now?"

Epilogue

Rachel stood at the rear of the crowded church, her bouquet in one hand, Samantha holding tightly to the other.

"Now?" the excited child asked.

"Very soon." Rachel smiled down at her. "Remember what you're supposed to do?"

"Uh-huh. I throw flowers and stuff. On the floor." Her blue eyes widened. "You sure I won't get in trouble?"

"Positive." Rachel laughed softly. "I'm the bride and I get to do anything I want today. Even make a mess in church so I can walk on flower petals."

"Okay." Samantha giggled. "I'm gonna do that when I'm a bride, too."

"I'm sure you will." Love glowed in Rachel's eyes as she looked from the child to the wonderful man who had just joined the pastor in front of the altar. "There's Sean. See? It's almost time. Are you ready?"

"Uh-huh."

Bending, she kissed the child's warm cheek, then took her by the shoulders, turned her so she'd be facing the right direction and made a last-minute adjustment to the circlet of fresh flowers atop her blond curls.

"Okay. The music is starting. Let's go. I'll be right behind you."

Watching the two most important people in his life approaching, Sean was in awe. Rachel's elegant white gown accentuated her delicate but regal stature, and her flowing skirt barely brushed the floor as she glided toward him.

Walking slowly in front of her and grinning from ear to ear, Samantha was taking evident pleasure in scattering handful after handful of rose petals. When a few of those petals fluttered down and landed outside the aisle runner, the little girl dutifully followed and stomped them flat with her brand-new patent leather shoes, bringing titters of laughter from wedding guests who were close enough to see what she was doing.

Samantha paid them no mind. As Sean watched, he saw her pause and lift her gaze to the highest part of the vaulted ceiling. Then she smiled, nodded and continued straight to the front of the sanctuary, where she reached for Sean's hand as if she'd just been reminded of the solemnity of the ceremony.

Those who had been observing her progress looked up at the empty rafters, then at each other, with curious interest.

Sean's gaze met Rachel's. Mutual understanding held it. They didn't have to wonder what Samantha had seen or heard. They knew she believed guardian angels had blessed her with a new family—and that was fine with them. After all they'd been through, they weren't about to question the simple, unshakable faith of their very special little girl.

*   *   *   *   *

Dear Reader,

I checked the cyclopedic index in my Bible and found sixty-seven listings concerning angels—and that's not counting the forty-seven more in the concordance!

I don't presume to understand everything about angels, but I do know Jesus spoke plainly about the jobs they do here on earth and in the heavens, and that's a good enough reference for me.

Could a child with a special need actually see an angel the way Samantha does in this story? I think so. Children had a special place in Christ's heart, and there's no reason to believe that has changed from then to now.

Have I ever actually seen an angel? Maybe I have and just didn't realize it. Either way, my faith is not based on things seen, as this story explains. Faith is a gift with two sides: intellect and choice. Each of us has the inner need to believe in a Higher Power, but that's only the beginning. Choosing to surrender to the will of God and follow Jesus is what makes the difference. That part of faith cannot be reasoned out like a puzzle; it can only be embraced wholeheartedly. That, I *am* sure of.

I'd love to hear from you. You can write to me at P.O. Box 13, Glencoe, AR 72539, check out my Web site at www.centurytel.net/valeriewhisenand/, or e-mail me at valw@centurytel.net.

Blessings,

Valerie Hansen

Love Inspired

TAKE MY HAND

BY

RUTH SCOFIELD

Being a single parent was more difficult than James Sullivan had expected, and he returned to his long-lost faith for guidance. But was his young son's teacher, Alexis Richmond, the answer to his prayers? And would their newfound love be strong enough to overcome Alexis's painful past and give her the family she'd always dreamed of?

Don't miss

TAKE MY HAND

On sale August 2003.

Available at your favorite retail outlet.

Visit us at www.steeplehill.com

LITMH

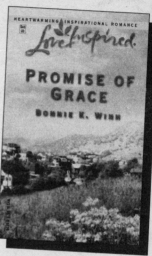